FLIGHT FROM FEAR

Tommy never wanted to come to Australia. After his mother and sister were killed in an air raid, all he wanted to do was to find his father—somewhere in Africa with the British Army. Instead he is sent to Australia to be looked after by his aunt and finds himself in Tiboorie.

To Tommy, Tiboorie is the end of the world, the middle of nowhere. Yet even here there's an Air Force base with its reminder of air raids and bombs...

FLIGHT FROM FEAR

Deirdre Hill

HODDER AND STOUGHTON
SYDNEY AUCKLAND LONDON TORONTO

I wish to thank my brother Flight-
Lieutenant Bob Curtis D.F.C. (RAAF
1942–46) for his technical assistance, and
to acknowledge that *Flight from Fear*
originated as a film script, initiated by
Jenifer Hooks, Merryweather Productions
Pty. Ltd.

First published in 1988 by
Hodder and Stoughton (Australia) Pty Limited
10-16 South St, Rydalmere, NSW 2116
© text, Deirdre Hill, 1988

National Library of Australia Cataloguing-in-Publication entry
    Hill, Deirdre, 1925–
        Flight from fear.
        ISBN 0 340 41935 0.
        I. Title. (Series: Stoat books).
    A823'.3

Typeset in 12/14 Baskerville by G.T. Setters Pty Limited
Printed in Singapore by Kyodo-Shing Loong Printing Industries Pte Ltd

CONTENTS

To
Anita

1   A NEW HOME

On a red-brown dirt road on the outskirts of a town called
Tiboorie, two boys rode their bikes. They rode past the
fenced green fields where cows grazed, past scattered gum
trees, the occasional iron-roofed house, sometimes riding
no-hands, sometimes weaving across the empty road.
They wore open-necked shirts and khaki shorts and they
were both eleven years old.

At the bottom of a shallow dip the road changed from
dirt to bitumen and on one side a high wire fence
stretched out into the distance.

Behind it stood rows of red-brick buildings and tall,
iron hangars. Aircraft of different shapes and sizes were
dispersed around the area, all painted with camouflage
designs and all with the large RAAF red, white and blue
circles on their sides.

They heard the drone of an aircraft engine and both
boys squinted into the sky.

"It's a Dakota," Peter called.

"No it's not, it's a DC3," his friend Charlie yelled
back.

"Charlie!" Peter groaned. "It's the same thing. You just don't know anything about aeroplanes."

They watched the plane come lower and lower—a big plane with windows down the side of the fuselage, two engines and a high tail. They watched it bank, turn and then come in to land, finally taxiing over to the line of buildings.

"I'm going to fly Spitfires," Peter announced proudly.

"War'll be over," Charlie said, sliding his bike to a halt.

Peter followed and they stood on the side of the road looking across the airfield.

"It could go on for six years more, easy. There are millions of Japs."

"You'll probably end up flying Zeros."

"What do you mean by that?"

"Well, if the Japs win we'll all be Japs."

"You say the silliest things sometimes, Charlie." Peter moved his bike nearer the fence to watch a Wirraway taxiing on to the tarmac for take-off.

Peter loved living near the Air Force station. His father was in the regular Air Force and had been stationed there for as long as Peter could remember—long before the war started. But now that the Japs had bombed Pearl Harbour, had captured Singapore and Rabaul and were heading for Australia, reinforcements were being sent north as fast as possible. Peter's father's job as Equipment Officer meant he had to see that supplies for the Air Force were flown north, that they were brought in and flown out as quickly as possible. It was an important job. With the enemy as far south as New Guinea everyone knew there might be an invasion of Australia, and work at the Air Force station was becoming heavier every day.

"My mum thinks the Navy's better," Charlie said, losing interest as the Wirraway flew out of sight.

"How can the Navy be better? *Zoom, wham.*" Peter demonstrated the manoeuvres of a fighter plane. "A stupid battleship can't do that."

"It's safer."

"Who wants to be safer?"

"I dunno," Charlie shrugged. "Mum I suppose."

"Well you can go into the middle of the ocean and do nothing," Peter told him. "I'm going up into the sky in a Spitfire."

"Race you home," Charlie called and he mounted his bike and rode off down the bitumen road.

Charlie was smaller than Peter and with his shock of fair, curly hair, looked younger. They lived near one another, went to school together, swam in the river and rode their bikes together.

As they rode along the road they passed the gates leading into the Air Force station. The guard on duty returned Peter's wave with a mock salute and as they rode on further they could see the town with its white-painted post office tower rising high above the other buildings. They couldn't see the clock, but guessed it was going on for five o'clock. Time to be home.

The warning bell was clanging loudly as they came to the railway crossing and they skidded to a stop. The gatekeeper walked out of his house and closed the gates across the road in front of them.

With legs straddling their bikes, they waited. Any moment the train would come around the corner at full steam. As it passed the crossing it would start hissing and spurting steam, with the brakes dragging on the wheels, slowing it down for the stop at the station.

It came towards them just as it always did—a black and red engine with smoke pouring out of its funnel, the driver pulling on the whistle. The carriages flashed past. The uniformed men of the RAAF were standing up ready to get out at the railway station. Some of the windows were open, people sitting there looking out. One of them, flashing by, was a young boy about their own age. His eyes met Peter's and then the train passed.

Peter stood for a moment before getting back on to his bike. Funny looking kid, he thought. Wonder where he's going? Oh, well, he'd never see him again, so why worry.

The railway station at Tiboorie looked like any other single-line country station. Clean white gravel on the concrete platform, a brown corrugated iron awning over the entrance of the waiting room and ticket office, some bedraggled pot plants, and one or two men and women waiting for the train to pull in.

The Tiboorie signboard had been taken down some months ago in case the Japanese invaded and now Australian train-travellers felt as lost as everyone hoped any invading Japanese would be. In April 1942 a trip through the Australian countryside by train, especially during the night, was not easy.

Mrs Walters had come to the station early, almost half an hour before the train was due. She was a thin, wiry woman wearing a light cotton frock patterned with flowers, a white hat with a blue ribbon band, shoes and stockings, and a white handbag hung over her arm. Her dark brown hair had little streaks of grey, but as it didn't come far past her ears, not much of it could be seen.

She looked anxiously down the line every minute or so, keeping one eye on the station master's office for any sign of his coming out with his flag and whistle ready for the train's arrival.

On the street behind the station a taxi pulled up. Two men wearing the dark blue uniform of RAAF officers climbed out and walked on to the platform. The taxi driver looked at his watch, got out of his car and leant against the front mudguard. He pushed his hand through his thick grey hair and he too looked down the line in the direction the train would come.

Not a cloud in the sky, hardly a murmur on the sun-drenched station. Everyone waited.

In the distance white puffs of smoke poured into the blue sky, a whistle sounded and the train came hissing towards the station. The people on the station stirred into action.

Mrs Walters walked a few steps along the platform, turned and looked back to see whether Jack Martin was waiting, saw that he was and, as the train moved slowly past her, she peered anxiously through each window.

At the far end of the train a woman and a boy alighted. Other passengers walked through the ticket barrier, but these two waited and Mrs Walters hurried up to them.

Nearing the boy, she stopped and asked cautiously. "Tommy?"

The woman with him answered. "You're Mrs Walters? Oh, what a trip! It's so hot. I'm Miss Hume from the department. We've talked so often on the phone I feel we've almost met. I do think Tommy ought to take his coat off."

Mrs Walters nodded, but kept looking across at the boy. "I'm your Auntie Marion, Tommy," she said quietly.

He took a step towards her and put out his hand.

She bent down, put her arms around him and hugged him to her—just for a moment. Then she stood up again and smiled. "You've come such a long way. But now you're here."

She kept smiling. "What about your coat?"

"I'd raver leave it on," he told her, his cockney accent very like her own.

He wore a grey woollen coat and pants, long thick socks and laced up boots. His cap perched high on the top of his head, unable to cope with the thick crop of wiry hair underneath it.

From behind them came the booming voice of Jack Martin as he crunched his way down the platform. "Well, he arrived all right, Marion. Not far to go now and you'll be home."

Mrs Walters gave him a warning look.

"It's a new home for him, Marion," Jack continued, "but home it is. Welcome to Tiboorie, Tommy. I've got my taxi waiting for you."

"Jack, this is Miss Hume from the Department of Child Welfare and Tommy Hooper, me nephew."

Jack Martin shook Tommy firmly by the hand and picked up the suitcase from the side of the platform. "It's a long way from England, Tommy," he said. "You'll be glad to finish with travelling."

They all walked towards the taxi. Jack Martin opened the back door for Mrs Walters and Miss Hume, put the suitcase in the middle of the front seat and Tommy climbed in beside it. They drove off down Station Street to the main road and sped along it towards Tommy's new home.

He sat silently next to Jack Martin in the front of the taxi while Miss Hume and Mrs Walters talked in the back. Miss Hume had looked after Tommy in Sydney for the few days from the time he'd left the ship to the day he'd caught the train. He had stayed in a house with a lot of other children, but gradually they had all left and gone off to the places where they would remain for the duration of the war.

"Got a grandson your age, Tommy," Mr Martin told him. "I'll bring him round to meet you. Peter—Peter Andrews—my daughter's boy."

Tommy looked out of the window at the flat paddocks, the cows, the gum trees. "Does he go to school?" he asked.

"Probably be in the same class. We'll drive past the school on the way."

He pointed out the various parts of the town as they drove by. The church, the school, the football ground. He pointed to the Air Force station right across the other side of the town, and explained that the district was a dairying one, mainly flat and lush with lots of cows.

"You lived in London, didn't you, Tommy?"

"Did once. Moved to Exeter we did, last year."

"You talk like a Londoner," Mr Martin remarked. "Your auntie still does too."

Tommy was about to ask if there was a picture show in the town, when Mr Martin pressed the horn on the steering wheel, tooted loudly and waved his arm out the window. "There's Peter," he called, "and young Charlie Calder."

The taxi passed the two boys pedalling furiously on their bikes, waving with one hand and desperately trying to keep up. Tommy saw that they were the boys who had been waiting at the railway crossing and turned his head to watch them disappear in the distance.

"There's Grandad," Peter shouted.

From the window of the taxi ahead of them a bare arm shot out and waved. Peter and Charlie rode as fast as they could, but gradually the distance between them and the car widened and they were left behind.

They relaxed and rode side by side and Charlie asked, "Who was the kid in your grandfather's taxi?"

"Didn't see him."

"He was in the front. Mrs Walters and another lady were in the back."

"Only saw Grandad."

The two boys parted at the crossroads. Charlie rode on to his house a few streets away and Peter leant against the fence outside his house to wait for his grandfather's taxi. He knew his grandfather would come home as soon as he'd dropped his passengers and Mrs Walters' shop was only a little way away. She and her husband used to run the petrol station and garage, but Mr Walters had joined the Army and been sent to Darwin. Now she just ran one petrol pump and a little shop next to it. Mostly lollies and cigarettes and cakes and things.

In a few minutes the taxi rolled to a stop in front of the house and Peter pushed his bike through the gateway and walked up the front path with his grandfather.

"Have a good ride?"

"We went out past the Air Force station. Grandad, who was the kid in your taxi?"

"Mrs Walters' nephew. Picked him up from the train. Tommy Hooper. Just arrived from England."

"How could he come from England? What about the war and the submarines and all that? How did he get here?"

"By ship. Had a rough time in the bombing. That's why he's here. You can ask him all about how he got here, when you meet him."

"When'll that be?"

"He'll be going to school with you. Your age."

Mr Martin walked up the steps to the veranda of the house and Peter wheeled his bike around the corner and went down the side of the house to the back. He thought about what his grandfather had said. He'd seen the bombing of London on the newsreel and heard about it on the wireless, and wondered whether this Tommy Hooper had really been there.

But a new kid at school? He didn't want anyone new. Things were all right as they were. He and Charlie and the others. Some of them were his friends, others weren't, but he didn't want anyone new. New kids meant all kinds of complications. A sudden quick thought went through his head, so quick he didn't really know it had been there. What if Charlie liked him better? No, Charlie wouldn't do that. But a new kid was a real nuisance.

He put his bike in the shed and his mother called. ''Don't put your bike away, Peter. I want you to go around to Mrs Walters' and get some butter.''

Peter sighed and wheeled it out again into the open, took the money from his mother and rode off back down the street.

2 UNKNOWN TERRITORY

Tommy and Miss Hume waited outside the shop while Mrs Walters fumbled in her handbag for the front-door key.

Miss Hume wanted to leave on the late afternoon train but had been persuaded to come inside for a cup of tea. In any case she had to put in a report when she got back to the city and she would need to include something about the house where Tommy was to live. Although he would be living with a close relative, the Child Welfare Department would keep in touch and help with any problems that might arise. Most of the children who had come to Australia from the cities of England had been sent to foster parents—people who had volunteered to look after them until the war was over.

Tommy had never really seen a house made all of wood before. It was painted white. Half the front was a shop and half a large garage with big swing-back doors and an awning over them. Concrete covered the whole of the front yard and a petrol pump stood under the awning. He supposed the house stood behind all this and when at last

Mrs Walters opened the door of the shop they all walked through a beaded curtain into the living room.

Miss Hume sat down and Tommy followed his aunt along the hall to a bedroom. She put his suitcase on to a bed in the middle of the room and turned to him, smiling. "Here we are, Tommy. A bit bare, but, once you get your things out, it'll be different. A room's got to be lived in."

They didn't speak for a few moments as he looked around him. Then she went on. "Will I open your suitcase now, Tommy, and help you put your things away? Or will we have a cuppa first?"

He didn't know what to answer. He didn't really care. There wasn't much to put away.

Each step he had made had taken him further and further into unknown territory and now, after six weeks of travelling he had arrived. He had gone from Exeter to London, London to Tilbury. The ship had taken him to Durban in South Africa, across the Indian Ocean to Australia—Perth, Melbourne, Sydney and now Tiboorie. They hadn't let him go to North Africa to be with his dad. That was what he wanted.

"I'll make a cuppa then." She fussed about the room for a moment. "Put your things into these drawers."

"Ta. Ah—."

She walked across to the door. "Call me Auntie, luv, or Auntie Marion if you like. We'll get on like a house on fire once you settle in. You'll like it here, Tommy. Your uncle and I were never sorry we left London, not for a minute in the whole twenty years we've been here. Twenty years ago, imagine that. Your dad wasn't much older than you when I said goodbye to him. He was me only brother, you know."

She went out of the door and he heard cups rattling in the kitchen. He liked the way she talked. The same as his mother. He turned away because his eyes smarted. They always did when he thought about his mother.

He undid the strap around his suitcase and opened the lid, put some of his clothes into the chest of drawers, then took out of the case a battered, charred book. He put it on the table beside his bed and walked to the window.

The country stretched out over green fields to a far-off line of hills. Green fields. But a different colour green and a sky much bluer. The few straggly trees were half brown, tired cows rested under them and the clouds in the deep blue sky shone with orange and red lights as the sun set behind them.

He opened the bedroom door, walked through the lounge, through the shop and out into the open. Tommy felt cold and hard inside as though a rock had been put into his chest.

He leaned against a post and watched a lone bike-rider coming along the road. He came nearer and nearer.

Outside the shop Peter slid his foot along the road and his bike came to a stop.

The two boys looked at one another—Peter with tanned skin, and short black straight hair and Tommy, pale with thick red-tinged hair that didn't stay down easily. A whole world between them.

"Shop's shut," Tommy said.

Peter stared and didn't speak.

"I'll get me auntie if you want somefing."

"What language do you speak?" Peter asked.

Tommy glared. "English."

"Well, I can't understand you."

Tommy turned towards the shop. "I'll get me auntie."

"Just a sec.," Peter called, "you're the new kid from England, aren't you? I saw you in the train."

"Used to live in England. Now I live 'ere wif me auntie."

"I bet you think it's better here."

"No I don't," Tommy shot at him. "It's not better at all."

"You've got bombs and everything in England."

"And you haven't got nuffin' 'ere."

"What do you mean, nothing?"

"Nuffin' 'cept cows and grass. It's empty."

"There's shops and there's houses," Peter told him looking around. "There's lots of things in town anyway."

"I 'aven't seen anyfing."

"Well you haven't looked."

"End of the earf."

Peter wheeled his bike to the side of the shop. "Are you going to call your auntie, or aren't you? I've got to get something for my mum."

Tommy walked past him and as he went to the door of the shop Peter called after him, "You talk funny—" then added as Tommy disappeared, "And your pants are too long."

Once inside the shop Tommy ran through the beaded curtain and followed the sound of clattering dishes to the kitchen. He told his aunt there was a customer outside, ran down the hall and flung open his bedroom door. Grabbing the clothes from his suitcase he stuffed them into the drawers, closed the case, put it on the ground and stood in the middle of the room.

"I'll show 'em," he said to himself. "England's better than this crummy old place. He thinks he's smart and he's not. He 'asn't got a picture palace and he 'asn't got a local and he 'asn't got nuffin'. Just grass and cows."

He heard his aunt calling.

"Tea's up, Tommy. Wash your hands in the bathroom first."

"Where's the stupid bathroom?" he muttered as he

walked out into the hall. He found it, washed his hands and went into the living room.

They had their cups of tea together and soon afterwards Miss Hume left for the station. Then they moved into the kitchen and Mrs Walters began preparing their meal.

"That was Peter Andrews that came into the shop, Tommy. I didn't have time to get you to meet him. He's Mr Martin's grandson. You know, the man who drives the taxi."

"Didn't like 'im much."

His aunt stopped what she was doing and looked across at him, astonished. "Why? Peter's a nice boy."

"Said I talked funny."

"Well now." She sat down on the chair next to him and drew in a deep breath. "Well now, that's just something you've got to live with here, Tommy. We're Londoners you and me. We talk cockney like our dads and mams and grandparents—way back. It sounds different to people here an' all."

"They're the ones what talk funny."

"Half the time they're talking cockney themselves and don't know it. You'll get used to them and they'll get used to you, my pet."

"Do I 'ave to go to school?" he asked.

His aunt put her arm tightly around his waist. "Of course you do, luv. It's all arranged for Monday."

She felt for him. She had come to this new country years before and there had been many bad moments. But she hadn't been alone. She had had Bert.

Charlie Calder arrived home and raced into the kitchen calling to his mother. She had a spoon in her hand and was beating something in a bowl. He stopped next to her and peered into it.

"What's for dinner?" he asked.

"Just wait," she told him. "I'm trying to talk to Tim."

Charlie looked across at his brother leaning against the dresser with a bunch of papers in his hand. Tim, almost eighteen, was an older edition of Charlie. Tall, fair curly hair, blue eyes, tanned skin but with a few freckles on his nose and cheeks. Both boys looked like their mother, but she was medium height, slim and pretty.

"There's a new kid in town," Charlie announced dramatically.

His mother kept on with her mixing and Tim groaned. "Will you let me talk to Mum?" he said.

"Just a sec. He was on the train. We saw him and then we saw him in Mr Martin's taxi with Mrs Walters."

"Oh." Suddenly Mrs Calder became interested. "That must be her nephew." She put down the spoon. "He was supposed to arrive from England ages ago. I almost forgot about it."

Charlie, delighted to find his news had created some interest, almost shouted. "From England! What's his name?"

His mother didn't know and Tim became tired of all the interruptions. "Will you just go and put your head in a bag for a while, Charlie?"

"Gosh, I come home with a great bit of news and nobody wants to listen."

His mother assured him she'd listen later and Tim, looking awkward, came up to the table and put his papers down.

"I've got to have a parent's signature, Mum. One signature."

"Mine?" she asked, her voice flat. She knew what the papers were and she had feared Tim's bringing them to her. He wouldn't turn eighteen until May and she had hoped that there would be no talk of his joining the Navy until then. But now he had his papers and if she signed them there would be nothing stopping his call-up.

She had asked herself what his father would have done and knew the answer. But his father had sailed with the Eighth Division to Singapore over six months ago. Now that Singapore had been captured by the Japanese, they had heard nothing more about him.

She was responsible for Tim, for his whole future and it all depended on her signing one small piece of paper.

She took up the pen.

Charlie had been standing by the sink watching. The prospect of his brother going into the Navy excited him, but in the back of his mind he still wondered why he chose the sea instead of the Army or the Air Force.

"Why don't you go into the Air Force, Tim? You could fly planes then."

Tim turned on him roughly. "Because I want to join the Navy, smarty. Mum, tell him to keep quiet."

She didn't need to. Charlie saw the look in his brother's eyes and decided himself that he wouldn't say any more. Anyway he was glad Tim was going into the Navy. No one else in Tiboorie had gone to sea.

"Can't you wait—just a while, Tim?" his mother asked.

"If I wait, conscription will come in. I don't want that, Mum. I want to volunteer—like Dad did."

Mrs Calder signed the paper.

"Oh boy," Charlie couldn't contain himself. "Now I'll have a father in the Army and a brother in the Navy. That's better than Peter. He's only got a father in the Air Force." He thought about it for a minute and added, "Gosh, Mum, you've only got to wait six years and all your family will be at the war."

The mixture in the bowl on the table swirled from one

side of the basin to the other as Mrs Calder beat it hard with the spoon. Tim put the papers into an envelope and tucked them into his pocket. Then he put his arm around his mother's shoulder.

"You'd better join the Air Force, Mum. Then there'd be one of us in each of the services. You'd look good in uniform."

Charlie sprang to attention and raised his hand to his forehead in a salute. "Morning, Sir, no, Mum—gosh, what would we call you if you did join the WAAAF?"

She poured the mixture into a dish and half smiled at them. "In that very unlikely event, Charlie, you'd call me Ma'am and I'd be giving the orders. Order number one. Charlie Calder clear that table and set it for dinner. Quick, on the double!"

She whisked some of the dishes on to the sink and Charlie went to the dresser drawer.

Tim walked to the door. "I'll just walk down to the post box, Mum, only be a tick." He walked outside with the envelope and her eyes followed him until he disappeared from sight.

3   FEELING ALL WRONG

Tommy's aunt took him up to the school at half past eight on Monday morning so that she would be back in time to open the shop at nine. He had expected to come home for lunch, or dinner as he called it, and when she packed his school-bag with something for mid-morning and sandwiches for lunch he picked up the packet and said, "Lunch? What abaht me dinner? Can't I come 'ome mid-day?"

His aunt cleared the breakfast table busily. "The children all stay at school mid-day," she told him. "Eat your sandwiches in the playground with the others. They sit under the trees."

"But I won't know no one."

"You'll get to know them. They're all nice children. You know Peter."

"Will I wear me coat?" he asked, ignoring the name, wondering what the other children would be wearing.

"I don't think you'll need it. It'll be a hot day." Then she looked at him, thinking. "I'll get you some new things later in the week."

He wore his grey short pants and a long-sleeved white

24

shirt and when he saw the other children in the playground he knew he was all wrong.

He stood with his aunt while she filled in some forms
with his new teacher, Miss Leslie, then he went to the
gate with her and watched her go down the street,
stopping to turn and wave every few steps. When he
could no longer see her he walked towards a row of seats
in the grounds.

A few children looked sidelong at him, keeping their
distance. Most of the area was asphalt, but there were
plenty of trees around the edge of the playground. He was
surprised to see sandbags over the entrances to the
buildings and paper strips over the glass on the windows.
He knew they didn't have air-raids.

When Miss Leslie came out of the main building, he
reluctantly decided that she looked much nicer than any
other teacher he'd ever seen. She didn't appear to be very
old and wore a light blue dress that waved around her in
the breeze. Her hair blew back from her face and reached
almost to her shoulders and she smiled a lot.

Everyone except Tommy stood around her and when
they all walked over to him, he stood up. He couldn't
remember all the names she told him—there was a Mary
and a Jean and a Ken and one of the other boys was
Frank. Peter wasn't there. When Miss Leslie left them
and went back into the school building, they stood
looking at one another, the girls giggling.

Tommy wondered if they were going to ask him to play
with them. One boy had a ball and someone else had a
bat. But they didn't.

"What you got all them sandbags for?" he asked. "I
fort there was no bombs 'ere."

Hands went up to faces as the girls giggled louder.

"There aren't."

"Might be one day," another boy volunteered.

"We 'ad real proper air raid shelters in our school."

"Where was that?" a girl wanted to know.

"Lunnun."

"Gosh, have you seen the King and Queen?" she asked.

"Lots of times."

"I don't believe you." Frank half turned away.

"Have so, and I seen Buckingham Palace too."

Mary looked at him carefully, from his laced up boots to his thick wiry hair. "What else have you seen?"

Tommy thought for a moment before answering. He'd tell them. He'd tell them something they didn't know anything about. "Tower o' Lunnun."

"What's that?" someone else asked, curious.

"It's where all the toffs got kept and tortured and got their 'eads cut off."

That was too much for the boys. "Aw. What are 'toffs' anyway?"

At the far side of the playground Peter rode through the open gate on his bike. Charlie rode behind him.

"Sir Walter Raleigh had 'is 'ead cut off there." Tommy's voice became louder. His audience was growing. "He was a toff."

"What's a toff?" Frank asked again.

"One of them people who don't 'ave to work to get their money. They're toffs. Like the King and Queen."

"Everyone works. They do here. Our Prime Minister said they had to because of the war. Anyway, if it was so good in England what did you come out here for?"

Peter and Charlie put their bikes in the bike racks and walked across to the crowd.

"Yeah," Peter said, joining them, "what did you come here for?"

The girls lost interest and moved away and Tommy looked around for the place he had had on the seat.

The boys chanted loudly. "Yeah. What did you come for if it was so good?"

Tommy saw the seat and made for it quickly. "I had to," he said and sat down.

"Come on, Peter," Frank called, "you can bat."

"I don't want to play cricket," Peter called, "I'm playing fighters. Come on Charlie. Bags being Bluey Truscott."

"Okay. I'm Killer Caldwell, then," Frank called.

A group joined together and they ran off making engine sounds in their throats and using their arms as wings.

The others raced over to the dry earth pitch they used for cricket.

Charlie stayed. "Are you going to live here?" he asked, sitting beside Tommy on the bench.

"Yes. Wif me auntie."

"Mrs Walters?"

"Yes."

"You'll be able to have as many lollies as you like."

"Might."

"Come on, Charlie." Peter beckoned with a wide sweep of his arm. "Who do you want to be?"

Charlie stood up. "You can play too if you like."

"No fanks." Tommy breathed in deeply. "I'll just . . . wait here."

And Charlie ran off to join the others.

When the school bell rang, the children marched into the classroom and stood beside their desks. Tommy stayed in front of the class, waiting. He knew Miss Leslie was trying to make things better for him, but she wasn't. As she talked to the class he felt he wanted to disappear right into the centre of the earth.

"I want you to meet your new classmate—Tommy Hooper," she said to the thirty children standing in front of her. "Tommy has come all the way out here from England." She stopped for a moment, expecting them to react, but they stood stony-faced. Some looked at her and some at Tommy, taking in his boots, his trousers that almost reached to the top of his long socks, his long-sleeved shirt, his hair that stood up and wouldn't sit flat on his head. This new boy was certainly not one of them.

"So I know you'll all help him as much as you can. Perhaps later on Tommy will tell us something about his experiences in England. Will you do that, Tommy?"

He nodded his head. "Yes, Miss."

"Miss Leslie," she corrected.

"Yes, Miss Leslie."

Then she showed him a seat next to a boy called Kevin and before they sat down the class repeated a prayer, mumbling the words.

"God bless our country, our king and our queen and all the brave men who are fighting our enemies in all parts of the world."

Suddenly Tommy wanted to tell them about his father, how he was fighting the Germans and the Italians in Africa. In his last letter he'd said that he was in Libya now, where there was desert and heat and fighting all the time.

But instead Tommy sat down, opened an empty, ruled exercise book and reached into his suitcase for his pen.

Mr Martin always bought his petrol from the Walters' garage, had done so from the time Bert Walters opened for business twenty years ago. Today he also wanted to find out how Tommy was settling in.

Jack Martin hadn't always driven a taxi. He was only doing that because the regular taxi driver was away at the war. He didn't have much of a petrol ration to keep things going. The small amount alloted to him each week was just about enough to take the townspeople to and from the railway station and the men from the Air Force station to and from various parts of the town. But he liked it. It was different from the job he had had before he retired. Then he'd been the editor of the local newspaper. A good job, where he'd had to know everything that was happening in the town. Now he still knew just about everything, not because he searched it out, but because his passengers told him. There wasn't much Jack Martin didn't know.

"Heard from Bert?" he asked Mrs Walters as she began to fill his petrol tank from the bowser.

She used a long-handled hand pump to bring the petrol from the underground tank, filled the bowser to the five-gallon mark and then released it off through the hose to the taxi's petrol tank.

"Got a letter yesterday," she replied. "Not that it told me much."

She took an envelope out of her apron pocket, removed the letter and opened it. It was full of cut-out holes like a paper doiley.

"Censor had a whale of a time." She laughed and folded it back again.

"Must have been telling you something about the bombing up there in Darwin," Jack Martin said. "No one's letting us know much about it. Wonder how they got on? Getting a bit close, Marion."

Mrs Walters agreed. People had been shocked when they heard that the Japanese had bombed the Australian mainland. Darwin! Singapore seemed a long way away. Rabaul, New Britain, New Guinea, were all distant places. But Darwin? That was right here in Australia.

"Well," she said, "if the Japs land there we might as well say goodbye to the rest of Australia."

"Doesn't bear thinking about, Marion," he said. Then straightening up from checking under the bonnet, he asked, "Tommy get off to school?"

"Yes, but he wasn't too happy?"

"Did he have a good week-end?"

"Settled himself in. We didn't do much. Got his books ready and things like that and I tried to get a bit of information out of him."

"You didn't tell us much about him, Marion. What's his history? Your brother's boy?"

"Yes. I didn't say much because I didn't know much. Me and me brother didn't write except at Christmas like. I knew he had two kids, Tommy and Essie, and when the war broke out I knew he joined the Army. Didn't hear much till he wrote and said he needed help, help with Tommy."

"What kind of help?"

"Someone to look after him. There wasn't anyone except his grandmother in London and she couldn't manage."

"What about the rest of the family? His mother and sister?"

"Got killed. Got killed in an air raid. Tommy was in hospital for months."

She took a handkerchief from her pocket and blew her nose. "That's why me brother asked me and that's why I said yes."

Mr Martin thumped his fist on the side of the car. "In London?" he asked.

"No. In Exeter. They was in the air-raid shelter in the garden of their home. They moved from London because of the raids there, and then this happens. Just when everyone thought they was going to be safe."

Jack Martin's eyes shone with anger. "Women and children! Don't you worry too much about Tommy, Marion. I'll keep an eye on him."

"I'm not used to children, Jack," she gave a little sniff. "Don't quite know what to do with them."

"He'll work himself out," he assured her, "and then there's Peter and Charlie. They're good lads. They'll help."

She took the hose from the car's tank and screwed on the cap.

"That'll leave you two gallons till the end of the week," she told him.

He opened the car door ready to get in and as he slid into the seat he called to her. "Marion! First thing you'd better do is get Tommy some new clothes. He's different enough without advertising it in that Pommy rigout of his. Give Margaret a ring. She might have something of Peter's."

4   TOMMY FINDS A BIKE

Each of the desks in the classroom seated two. Peter and Charlie sat together not far from Tommy and Kevin. Miss Leslie had given them a lesson on the early explorers and now the whole class was drawing a map of Victoria and the Murray River in their mapping books.

Tommy had liked hearing about Captain Sturt and his trip down the Murrumbidgee River, but he found it hard to spell the names of the places.

It was very quiet in the room and quiet outside too. The sound of an aircraft approaching, at first a dull, distant hum, then a louder drone, sounded rather like a summer blowfly. Peter looked out the window, craning his neck to see what it was. Probably a Beaufort coming in to land. Or it might be an American Lockheed Hudson.

He couldn't see it through the small opening of the window, so he listened for a moment to the roar of the engines as it came low down over them, concluded it was a Beaufort, and went back to work.

Kevin noticed Tommy first. He felt him stiffen beside him and then saw that he had pushed his pencil right through the page of his book. Then he began to shake. The whole class raised their heads and stared in disbelief when Tommy, his hands over his ears, slid down under the desk. He crouched on the floor in a tight ball, his head between his knees and his eyes shut tight, his body shaking.

Miss Leslie moved quickly towards him and Kevin slipped off his seat and squeezed in next to Peter and Charlie.

No one said a word. They stared.

Gently Miss Leslie tried to pull Tommy to his feet, speaking to him quietly. "What is it, Tommy? The aeroplane? It's just a transport, Tommy. It's landing at the airfield. It won't hurt you. Listen. It's gone."

Tommy stayed on the floor, shaking.

"It's gone," Miss Leslie repeated and slowly Tommy unwound himself and came back on to his seat. He put his head on the desk and his arms around his head. Miss Leslie sat next to him and waited.

In a few moments Tommy put his hand into his pocket, pulled out a handkerchief and rubbed it over his face.

"We'll go and wash your face," she said to him, just to him, and standing beside him she turned to the class.

"Go on with your maps everyone. Outline the rivers in blue pencil and nobody—" she stopped for a moment, looked across the sea of faces and repeated the word, "—nobody will speak."

Nobody did as she and Tommy walked out of the room and down the corridor. They returned a few minutes later, the edges of Tommy's hair wet and his face red and blotchy.

Not a head moved as Tommy came into the room. Pencils raced across the pages of the books, but one or two, out of the corner of their eyes, looked at him curiously and wondered.

The bell rang and the class spilled out into the play-ground, some finding friends so they could walk home together, others collecting their bikes. Tommy walked straight to the gate and knew that nobody would speak to him.

He felt angry. Angry with them, angry with himself, angry that he had done what he did when the aeroplane flew past. He'd done it before—back in England, on the ship, and once in Sydney. He just wished he would stop. He didn't want to shake, he knew the planes were only big transports. The German bombers were thousands of miles away. And the Japs weren't anywhere near either. He knew all that, but it made no difference. It just happened.

Everyone acted as though they didn't know he was there. They moved past him, crossed the road, talked and shouted around him. An invisible island, a tree, some-thing they didn't understand. It was much easier to pretend that he wasn't there than risk a face-to-face encounter. What could they say?

He was glad they didn't talk, because then he didn't have to answer and he hated them all.

On the path they used as a short-cut through a paddock to the next road, Charlie stopped and waited. Well—Charlie's not so bad, Tommy thought and slowed down to see what he wanted.

"Want to come swimming?" Charlie asked. "You all right?"

Tommy looked ahead and saw Peter leaning against his bike watching. He imagined that they would be going down to the river, the one his aunt and he had walked to on Sunday, but it was quite a way.

"Where abahts?" Tommy asked, squinting into the sun.

"Down the river."

Peter called. "He can't come. He hasn't got a bike."

"'Ow do you know I 'aven't?"

"Well, where is it, then?"

He would have liked to tell a lie and say he had one in the garage shed, but he didn't. Then while he was wondering if there might be one among all the bits of cars and things in there, Charlie said he'd double him if he liked.

It might have worked if it hadn't been for Peter who began to ride off.

"Come on, Charlie," he called, "it'll be dark before we get down there."

Charlie stood between the two, looking at Peter, then back at Tommy. He moved to follow Peter. "Want to come?" he asked again.

Peter wheeled his bike around and rode back past them. "He's too scared." And he circled around them.

"I'm not the one who's scared. Everyone else round here's scared." Tommy twisted around to follow Peter's slow taunting ride.

"Sez who?"

"What you got sandbags for when you haven't got a war?"

"We'll have a war. The Japs'll come. They're coming now."

Charlie, holding his bike upright, not sure whether to get on or not, tried to get in Peter's way so he'd ride off the path. Peter dodged.

"The Germans are only just across the Channel from England. Only twenty miles away. When I was there you could almost see them over the water." He stopped, thrusting out his jaw, but all he heard was Peter's, "Haw."

"The Japs are thousands of miles from 'ere."

Peter put one foot on the ground and faced Tommy.

"No one around here's scared," he said. "Anyway my dad's in the Air Force. He's over at the RAAF station."

"He's not fighting anyone. My dad's in Africa fighting the Germans."

Charlie joined in. "My dad fought the Japs."

"Yeah." Peter supported his friend, remembering the story of Charlie's father. "Charlie's dad's in Singapore and they don't even know if he's alive or anything."

It was time to go. Tommy swung his suitcase and walked past the two boys, but Peter called out.

"What about in school today? Who was scared of a blinking Beaufort?"

Colour rushed to Tommy's face and he felt the roots of his hair tingle. "I wasn't scared." He looked back at them and shouted. "I don't like the noise, that's all. It's the noise."

The quiet hung about them. No one spoke. Peter rode off down the path. Charlie put his foot on the pedal and swung his leg over the bar.

"See you down there if you want a swim," he said, and rode off behind Peter.

Miss Leslie had rung Mrs Walters and told her about Tommy's day at school.

"Surely someone must have realised that this town is almost next door to an Air Force station." She was distressed. "He's terrified of the noise."

It was something Mrs Walters hadn't imagined might happen. Of course he wouldn't like the sound of the aeroplanes, not after all the air raids he'd been through. She knew that when she thought about it, but the problem now was what had to be done.

She didn't disagree when Miss Leslie said she'd ring

the welfare people in Sydney and try to speak to Miss Hume, but she did think that, given a little time, she and Tommy could cope with it themselves.

She was in the kitchen when he came home and he could tell by her face that she already knew.

"They don't come over very often, luv," she said. "They fly around a bit, but the station's right over the other side of town. They don't seem to fly over here much at all."

He sat down on the kitchen chair and put his case on the floor beside him. "I can't help it, Auntie Marion."

"I know you can't, Tommy. No one's saying you should. I don't want you upset like this. But I can't stop them from flying. Here, have some milk. I'll get the biscuits."

She hurried over to the pantry and brought out a tin, pulled off the lid and put it on the table. "What if we don't worry too much about it now, eh? Give it time. You won't know yourself in a while with all the sun and the open air. You'll forget, Tommy."

He took a biscuit from the tin and held it in his hand near the edge of the table, looking down at it as he said, almost in a whisper, "No, I won't, Auntie. I won't forget."

She couldn't find words. His face was filled with pain and sadness and hurt.

She reached across and put her hand on his shoulder. "You won't forget your lovely mam and little Essie. No, darlin', you won't forget. But it'll fade just a bit. You'll learn to cope. I don't know how, but," she nodded her head, "you'll learn to live with it."

He began to eat the biscuit, and Mrs Walters, feeling helpless and inadequate, searched for something else to talk about, and remembered the delivery of sweets she'd received earlier in the day.

"I got a sweets delivery today," she said. "Everything's got to be put away in the jars. Thought you might help me."

Out in the shop he filled the first jar with sunbeams, little rounds of chocolate covered in hundreds and thousands, then the next with black striped humbugs, then another with chocolate frogs.

They worked together, not saying much.

"We 'ad ration cards for our sweets. But there wasn't many anyway," he said, concentrating on his job.

"It'll be the same here soon," she answered. "What with all this other rationing. Only essentials from now on."

"Lollies is essentials," he said.

She laughed with him and they relaxed. "How about a humbug?" She offered him the jar.

He pulled out one and sucked as he talked. "That Peter fair gets up me hooter."

"Peter Andrews?"

"'E's always talking about war and playing games about it. He don't know nuthin' abaht it."

"What about Charlie? Now, there's a nice boy."

"Charlie's all right."

"You could've gone over to play with him after school."

"Gone swimming."

"Well now, there you are. That's where you can go. Just whenever you like. I showed you the place last Sunday."

He moved the humbug from one side of his mouth to the other and drew in his breath before he spoke. "Auntie, do you fink..."

"Yes, luv?"

His words rushed out. "Do you fink somewhere there might be a bike?"

She dropped the box in her hands down on to the counter with a bang.

"What've I been thinking of? A boy can't live in Tiboorie without a bike."

"If we bought one, I could work in the shop for you and sweep it and do all that." His enthusiasm began to mount. "And save up."

In a second she was out of the shop calling to him to follow. She strode across the concrete towards the garage. Tall, thin and strong, she pulled open the heavy doors with a flourish. "Now why wouldn't there be a bike in here somewheres?"

She pushed aside some sheets of iron and knocked over a kerosene tin. "There's about everything else. Bert meant to clean all this mess up before he left," she went on, "but he got his letter one day and was gone the next."

She threw some boxes out from the sides to the centre and they searched together. "Can you ride a bike, luv?" she asked, her voice muffled from behind a pile of sacking.

"Yes, I 'ad one in Exeter."

"Well, that's a start."

"It got bombed though," he added.

She stopped for a moment, then began moving things aside again. "Now what's this?"

He raced over and helped her pull and lift out the frame of a bicycle—good condition, but no wheels.

"They must be somewhere 'an all," he shouted, pulling out bits and pieces, looking on the beams running across the roof of the shed. "I knew Uncle Bert'd 'ave one."

She stood back, looking at it. "I can remember now. He rode it—oh, years ago. Said he could go places on it cars couldn't get to. Liked fishing, my Bert."

"Auntie," he reminded her, "keep looking."

They found them in a corner right at the back. Both tyres flat, but they looked all right.

"I can easy test 'em for punctures," he said to her. "I've seen the other kids do it at home."

"Well now, there we are. Is everything here? Handlebars. There's a front-wheel brake, *hmm*, cord's disappeared, two pedals, chain. What else do we need?"

"Nuffin'," he said, looking at all the parts carefully. "It just 'as to go togever."

"Jack Martin's the person to do that," she said firmly. "He'll be coming over to fix on some blackout headlights in a couple of days."

Tommy's face fell. "Peter's grandfather?"

"That's the one. Come on now," she put her arm around his waist and they walked towards the open door, "Peter's not that bad."

"He's not that good neither," he said, helping her shut the door. "Hasn't Charlie got a grandfather?"

She laughed. "Only Peter. And he's a good friend of mine. Good friend of everybody's."

They went back into the shop and finished their job putting the boxes outside the garage and lining the shelves with the jars. Everything sparkled in the afternoon sun. The silver-paper wrappings, the red-and-gold paper covers on the bigger chocolates, the golden covered chocolate roughs. The display under the glass counter glittered.

Tommy looked at it all with satisfaction. If he were just a bit older he could stay and look after the shop all day. That was something he'd really like. He'd never ever have to go outside then, just look after the shop.

"What day's Mr Martin coming?" he asked as they walked out into the living room and through to the kitchen.

"We'll see him at the picnic on Saturday, Tommy, if I don't see him sooner. We can ask him then."

"Yes, but," he hesitated for a moment, "tell him not to tell that Peter."

5   PICNIC

It seemed to Tommy that every customer that walked into the shop during the week talked about the picnic. Sometimes after school he'd sit in the living room and listen to the sound of the voices coming through the bead curtain. His aunt must have known everyone in Tiboorie. She knew where their sons were, whether they were in the Army or the Air Force, what the daughters were doing and whether or not they were going to the picnic.

If the bike had been fixed he could have ridden it down to the river and ridden it when he got there, but he didn't have it. Mr Martin wasn't coming to look at it until Sunday.

He had begun to play with some of the other boys at school, avoiding Peter as much as he could, but—how was he going to go to a picnic by a river and not go swimming? He'd seen them all there when he walked down that day with his aunt, but he had never been in the water and never intended to. Not in a river, the sea or a swimming pool. He remembered one good thing and that was he didn't have a bathing costume, but his aunt took this excuse from him. She walked into the living room on

Friday and dumped a pile of parcels on to the lounge. Among all the new clothes she had bought for him was a swimming costume, red trunks with a smart white belt. She smiled with pleasure as he tried everything on.

The next morning they walked down to the river carrying their picnic basket between them. On the side of the river family parties had grouped themselves on rugs under the trees. Small children were playing on the river banks and the older ones were swinging into the brown muddy water from the overhanging branches or swimming around with their friends.

It looked hard and harsh to Tommy. Different from the parks of London and the riverside at Exeter with the soft green banks, the carefully laid-out paths and the garden beds filled with flowers.

Marion Walters waved to a group under a nearby tree and Jack Martin stood up and walked across to her, taking the basket. He introduced Tommy to everyone there—Peter's mother and father, Charlie's mother, and a few other people who seemed to be relations. He noticed both Peter and Charlie down on the river bank waiting their turn to climb the tree.

"Take off your shorts, Tommy," his aunt told him, and smiling at the others she said, "He's got his trunks on underneath."

Tommy sat down. "Will in a tick." He sat doodling with a twig on the sandy patch next to him, occasionally looking down at the river and wondering inside him what he would do. They could all swim, even the very small ones.

"Come on Tommy, you'll miss the best part of the day," his aunt called when she stopped her conversation for a moment.

"Might be a bit of a risk with that cold of his," Jack Martin said, standing up and walking over to Tommy.

"How about helping me get some wood. We'd better be putting the billy on soon or there won't be any tea for lunch."

Mrs Walters, surprised, opened her mouth to speak, but Jack Martin stood beside her, pressing against her arm with his foot.

She looked up at him for a moment, then at Tommy and then at the river. "Oh. Yes. Yes, Jack. I forgot about his cold for the minute. You'd better help with the wood, luv."

In the bush further up the hillside, the two worked at picking up sticks of wood and piling them into bundles in their arms.

"Not much swimming in your neck of the woods, eh Tommy?" Mr Martin asked.

"Water's made for drinkin' and washin'."

"Never swum in the sea?"

"No. We never went to the seaside. Yes, we went to Brighton once, but it were cold. I've seen a lot of sea now—every day like, for six weeks. But I don't want to swim in it."

"Do you want to learn?"

"No, not likely."

With their arms filled with sticks they turned to go back and as they walked Mr Martin said, "Well Tommy, it's April now. They'll only be swimming for a couple more weeks. Maybe your cold will last that long."

"I'll make sure it do, Mr Martin," Tommy said and grinned. "Aunt Marion got a surprise about me cold."

They built a fire and put on the billy and one by one the others came up from the river—Peter's sister Pam, Charlie's brother Tim, Charlie and Peter and a few boys Tommy had seen at school.

Willing hands spread tableclothes on the grass. Food spilled from baskets—sandwiches, cakes, biscuits, pikelets, fruit, cups, glasses and soft drinks.

Jack Martin threw the tea leaves into the boiling water, clamped on the billy's lid and knocked the side firmly with a stick.

He poured the light amber steaming liquid into the cups and Tommy handed them around. Then everyone began to eat.

"Coming in after lunch?" Charlie asked Tommy, but it was more a statement than a question.

His mother heard and spoke to him firmly. "Not for half an hour after your meal. At least half an hour, Charlie."

Charlie's mother, Mrs Calder, was the prettiest there, Tommy thought, except for Pam, Peter's sister, who was sitting with Tim. She had short black curly hair and wore a blue bathing costume. She was talking to Tim as though she might never seen him again.

"Tim's going into the Navy soon," Charlie told Tommy. "He's sent in his papers."

He'd identified just about everyone. Peter's mother was fatter than Charlie's and her hair was twisted into a bun. Mrs Calder's was light brown and wavy and pretty. He thought Peter's father looked like a really important Air Force officer, even though he wasn't wearing a uniform. He didn't smile very much.

Tim he liked. He wondered why he wanted to join the Navy with the sea so far away and the Air Force station so close. He asked him when Pam stood up to help her mother cut the cakes.

"Because I like the water," Tim told him. "See that river? Well, I've spent half my life on it, or in it. I've canoed on it and swum in it, half lived on it. I like boats and ships—so, it's the Navy."

"Didn't know Australia had a Navy," Tommy said.

"Course we have. Cruisers and destroyers. Not as many as England, but it's a pretty big Navy."

"Will you fight the Japs?"

"I suppose so."

"Your dad's in Singapore, isn't he?"

"Was when we last heard. We think he's a prisoner-of-war now."

"Don't you know?"

"Japs haven't told anybody who the prisoners are and who—" He stopped and looked across to see if his mother was listening. "—and who got killed."

Tommy saw him look at her and said quickly. "If your dad's a prisoner-of-war you can go up in a Navy ship and rescue him."

Tim smiled. "Might even be able to do that." He stretched out on his back, his hands behind his head. "First I've got to get into the Navy, then I've got to get on to a ship. Might give me a land job."

They lay in the sun after the picnic lunch, the boys keeping a close watch on the time. But as it neared two o'clock Jack Martin announced he was going up to see his sister and brother-in-law on the farm not far away. Some of their land stretched down to the river.

"Can you wait till we have a swim, Grandad?" Peter asked. "Then we'll come with you."

"Have your swim and come on later," he answered. "Plenty of time."

He beckoned to Tommy and they walked together away from the river, through the green paddocks, up a slight hill to the farm. The dairy sheds stood at the back facing the river, then came the farmhouse, and in front of it the big yard where fowls, ducks and a few other small animals roamed about. A long drive lined with pine trees stretched down to the road.

A man about the same age as Jack Martin leaned on the dairy fence and waved to them as they approached.

"Hello there, Bob," Jack called out. "Got a visitor for you."

Tommy noticed the milking stalls, the brick paved floor, and saw a darker and much younger man hosing the floor on the other side of the building.

"So long as you've brought a few pairs of milking hands, that's all right with me," Bob Turner called back.

"I'll give you a hand for a bit. Don't think Tommy here'll be much use to you yet. Just out from England."

"Hello there, lad. Heard a bit about you. There's a new litter of kittens in that shed there if you'd like to see them."

Tommy ran into the shed and watched the kittens pushing and prodding their mother to get to her milk, ran out again to join the two men and watched them replacing some fencing near the big gate. Bob Turner showed him some of the places where the hens laid their eggs and he searched around the yard, found four eggs and took them carefully into the kitchen of the house.

Mrs Turner stopped rolling out some pastry on a big wooden board and showed him where to put them, then rubbed her floury hands together and reached into a box and pulled out an apple for him. She knew who he was, even before he told her his name.

Outside again he ran across the yard to where the farmer had stopped to fill up the hens' water dishes. A group of ducks came flapping over and Tommy jumped aside in a hurry.

Bob Turner pushed them with his foot. "Wait a bit," he said. "You'll get yours. Greedy beggars they are."

"Can I help feed them?" Tommy asked. "I used to feed ducks once. In Kensington Gardens."

"Been to those gardens," the farmer told Tommy, "me and Jack back in the war. First World War. The Great War we called it. Saw a statue of Peter Pan there."

"We used to look at that too. And we fed the sparrers just near there on a little bridge. Put seeds on our 'ands, and then we'd 'ang ahrand and they'd come and peck it off. Right on our 'ands they'd stand, pecking away.''

They heard Jack Martin shout out from the direction of the milking sheds and looked across.

"Cows coming up, we'd better get ready for the milking.''

They hurried into the dairy as the cows came meandering up the hillside from the river. The man he had seen earlier in the afternoon walked behind them with another man, dark like the first, but taller.

They put the cows into the yard, Mrs Turner came out from the house and the first cows went into the stalls to be milked. They milked by hand but Tommy heard the farmer talking about milking machines coming in a few weeks. They were short-handed with the Turners' son Bill at the war, and butter was urgently needed to send off to England.

Peter and Charlie started climbing over the dairy fence and Tommy felt a wave of disappointment when he saw them.

"Want to see some kittens?'' he asked as they jumped down on to the ground from the fence.

"Where's everybody?'' Peter asked.

"Milking.''

"I don't want to see any dumb old kittens. Come on Charlie, let's see Grandad.''

Peter ran off but Charlie went into the shed with Tommy. He picked up one of the kittens, patted it, then put it down and ran off after Peter. "Come and see the milking,'' he called.

Tommy wanted to watch the milking, but not while Peter was there so he bent down and looked at the little kittens lying tightly together. He'd never seen anything so perfect. Little feet and tails, tiny eyes still closed, they twisted their bodies moving closer to the comfort of their mother. At last he stood up to go and there, in front of him, blocking the whole of the doorway, stood a huge, dark-faced jersey cow.

"*Shoo!* you can't come in 'ere. *Shoo!*" Tommy backed against the wall. He could hear the others outside and Jack Martin calling.

"Come on Tommy, hurry up. We need a hand."

"I can't come," he shouted back. "There's a great 'airy cah in the doorway."

He looked for an escape. No window, just walls.

Peter peered over the back of the cow. "Push her between the eyes."

Tommy took a step closer. How was he going to do that? He'd never been so close to an animal so big.

"You pull her," he shouted to Peter.

Peter disappeared and Tommy looked around in desperation. He found an old broken stool, picked it up and pointed it towards the cow.

"*Shoo!*" he yelled, thrusting the stool towards the placid face in front of him.

The cow moved slightly, backing out. Tommy felt a surge of power, like a bullfighter. He jabbed the stool at the cow again, and the heavy body moved further back. Tommy advanced, wielding the stool and gradually the cow backed out, swished her tail and plodded off towards the yard.

The small, dark man slapped the cow on the rump and she hurried off.

"You okay, boy?" he asked.

"I am now," Tommy answered, "but I can do wivout that cah."

The man laughed and went back to the dairy, Tommy following.

"Is a brava boy," he announced to the others in his Italian accent.

Tommy wondered who the man was. No one told him.
Peter was washing out a bucket at the tap and Charlie was
way over the other side of the shed helping Mrs Turner.
Tommy was pretty sure how the cow had got into the
doorway but just walked past Peter to the safety of the
fence, and climbed to the top. There he stayed till they'd
finished the milking and the cows were let out into the
paddock for the night.

It took a while to clean up the dairy after the milking.
The men poured most of the milk into big tin cans to be
sent to the factory and took the rest across to the farmhouse.

Before they left, the three boys had big glasses of thick
warm milk. Charlie gulped his down, but Tommy really
didn't like his very much. He preferred it cold and not so
full of cream.

They all walked back to the picnic area and found
everyone packing ready to leave. Tommy noticed Miss
Leslie in a group of people not far from them and he
wondered whether she had been talking to his aunt while
he was away.

It worried him to think of other people talking about
him. He knew they did and it gave him a sick feeling
inside. He didn't want to think back and he didn't want
to think forward. He was here now. He had come to this
country because he had to and he'd stay because he had
to. There was just nothing else he could do.

But there was one good thing. Mr Martin would be
around the next day to start fixing the bike.

6 SHARED GRANDFATHER

After the morning service at the little stone church in Tiboorie, the Andrews family walked home, Pam lagging behind with Tim. He had been invited to Sunday dinner and Pam knew that now every minute they had together was precious.

Mrs Andrews had left the roast in the oven while they'd been away and now she hurried in to the kitchen, pulling an apron on over her church clothes. She stoked the wood fire carefully.

The house they lived in was timber, like most of the other houses in the town and had a long veranda across the front with stone steps leading up from the garden. Peter's room was at the back. He went out there to change his clothes, taking as long as he could because he knew he'd be the one helping his mother, not Pam.

At least it was a bit better than being out on the veranda watching them holding hands, so he wandered into the kitchen and offered to set the table.

After the meal Peter's grandfather hurried off to his room and came back wearing the old clothes he kept for working in the garden or fixing the taxi.

Peter dried the dishes as quickly as he could, expecting his grandfather to call him to go with him—wherever he was going. But he didn't. Through the window Peter saw him go to the garage, pick up a few boxes, wave goodbye and drive off.

"Gosh, where's Grandad going?" he asked.

His mother scrubbed the bottom of a saucepan. "He's going to put on his blackout headlights. Using Mrs Walters' tools."

Peter slowed down at the wiping-up, feeling disappointed and hurt. He had wanted to watch how the blackout headlights were put on—he nearly always spent Sunday with his grandfather. Now he was left with nothing to do.

Jack Martin drove down the road towards Mrs Walters' garage feeling guilty. He enjoyed having Peter with him and they often went out on Sundays. But Tommy had specially asked him not to tell Peter about the new bike, so he had no alternative.

He'd have to do the headlights first. All cars had to have them on by 30 April. He had sent away for some, feeling that the exercise was really a waste of time. The covers for the headlights had slits which would throw the beam down on to the ground.

"Lot of nonsense," he said to himself. "Wouldn't be surprised if more people get killed on the roads than by the Japs."

He didn't believe that the brown-out would make much difference. But it had to be done, so he'd do it. Wouldn't take long and then he could get on with Tommy's bike.

They worked together in the garage. Tommy handed Jack the tools as he put the covers over the headlights of the taxi, but he was impatient to get on with the bike.

At last Jack could turn on the headlights to see how the covers worked.

"Do you think the Japs'll drop bombs 'ere, Mr Martin?" Tommy asked, looking at the slits of light through the covers.

"Possible, I suppose. Hand me that spanner, Tommy, and I'll just give this a twist. Hard to tell what's happening up north."

"The Germans dropped bombs on us in England. What did they do that for, Mr Martin?"

"If I knew, Tommy," he answered, giving a nut a hard jerk, "I'd be a wiser man that I am now."

"You went to England in the Great War, didn't you?"

"Yes. Me and my brother. Different kind of war then Tommy. We fought in trenches. Dug them ourselves out in the fields. Fifteen feet deep and they stretched for miles. Enemy only a few hundred yards away from us some of the time."

"Germans?" Tommy asked.

"Yes, Germans then, Germans now. What with them and the Italians and the Japs and the English and the French and the Russians and the Americans—all killing each other because of greed, or power or land! Things you and I don't know much about, Tommy." He turned around and picked up the bike. "Hey, how about handing me that wheel. About time we got going at putting all this together."

He stood back and looked down at the pieces of the bike lying where Tommy had spread them on hessian sacking. "Doesn't look a bad bike."

Tommy stood beside him staring out in front of him. "I'm going to fight 'em. I'm going to fight them Germans."

"You probably will one day," Jack Martin said, turning the wheel in his hands. "The way we're going there'll be no stopping it. Not much use talking. Men have got to learn a lot more sense before wars'll stop."

"My dad's going to make them sorry for...for...
everyfink they've done."

Jack Martin put down the wheel and looked carefully
at the tyre. "We'd better get on with our job, hadn't we,
Tommy? Hand me that lever over there and I'll get this
tyre off."

Tommy handed it to him and watched the tyre come
away from the rim of the wheel. "Does anyone besides
Peter want wars, Mr Martin?"

"Peter?" Jack Martin stopped pulling at the tyre.
"Why do you say, Peter?"

"He acts like it."

"We-e-e-ll." It was a long, drawn-out word as Mr
Martin thought about Tommy's remark. Then he asked,
"Why do you think he does that?"

"Because he's never seen a war. That's why."

Jack Martin took the tyre off and put the pieces on the
floor. He busied himself with the work, Tommy passing
him the tools, doing all the odd jobs and at last he asked
impatiently, "How long'll it take, Mr Martin?"

"Couple of hours. But then we've got to paint it, and
there are a few things I've got to buy for it. Do that next
week. What colour do you want it?"

Tommy looked at the pieces and glowed with excitement as he imagined it all together, shimmering and
glittering with new paint.

"I'd like it red and gold like a Nestles' chocolate. Red
down here with gold lines here." He pointed to the body
of the bike. "Can we do that?"

"We can try, Tommy."

They worked till five o'clock and then they leaned it up
against the garage wall and walked out into the daylight.
There, standing beside the electricity pole on the side of
the road, was Peter.

Mr Martin didn't notice him at first, not until he began

to pull open the doors of the garage to drive his taxi out. "How long have you been there?" he called.

"Couple of minutes. Wondered where you were," Peter answered.

Tommy helped with the doors, not saying anything, but hoping that Peter wouldn't notice the bike. He didn't want anyone to see it until it was ready and painted.

Peter walked towards them. "Did you fix the headlights? Let's see."

"Hold on now, I'll drive out," Mr Martin said, going into the garage. He sat behind the wheel and slammed the car door shut. Then he started the engine, reversed and drove on to the concrete drive.

Peter examined the headlights. "That all they are? Took a long time."

His grandfather kept the engine running and leaned out of the window. "Did you ride over?"

"No, I walked. We've been playing cricket on the oval."

"Hop in and we'll drive home."

Peter looked back at the garage. "I'll shut the doors for you," he said to Tommy.

Tommy raced over to the doors and began to shut them as quickly as he could, calling out that there was no need for Peter to help, he could manage. By the time Peter had come around to the other side of the taxi, he had closed the doors shut.

Peter looked at Tommy suspiciously, gave him a quick, "Bye", and got into the car. It rolled out towards the road with Mr Martin calling to Tommy through the open window to be sure and thank his aunt and tell her he'd see her again early in the week.

Tommy waved and with the car out of sight, went back into the garage.

Peter settled himself on to the car seat and looked out

of the window. At the corner of the street he turned to his
grandfather.

"We've got enough time to go down to the oval,
haven't we?" he asked. "Could you give us a few
bowls?"

"A bit late."

"I've been waiting for you the whole afternoon. Why
didn't you take me?"

"Don't take you everywhere now, do I? Didn't think
you'd want to spend an afternoon with Tommy Hooper.
You haven't been giving him much of a time."

"He's a show-off."

Mr Martin turned the last corner before home. "He's
trying hard to fit in. It's a bit different out here."

Peter pulled at the fingers of his hand. "You're my
grandad. Not his."

The taxi neared the house and Mr Martin eased it to
a stop. He sat quietly, looking hard at Peter. "I think I
can spread myself round a bit," he said and reached
across to open Peter's door. "Not enough fathers to go
round these days, let alone grandfathers."

Peter stepped out on to the footpath and his grandfather followed. "Give him a chance, Peter," he said,
joining him and ruffling his hair affectionately. "Give
him a chance."

A week passed before Mr Martin found time to come and
paint the bike. Tommy went off to school each day and
the boys who played cricket included him in the team.
First he fielded, then they let him bowl and he found he
could bowl as well as any of the others.

It took Mr Martin a long time to paint the fine lines of
gold on the bike once the main red had been put on, so
long that Tommy began to wish he hadn't asked for it.

"We'll have the first run on Saturday morning," Mr Martin announced. "Should be dry by then. What about asking Peter and Charlie to come over?"

"Do I have to?"

"No, you don't have to. Thought it might be a good idea, that's all." He waited. "Come on, we'll ask them," he said firmly, "and we'll have a big launching."

"Like a ship?"

"Without the champagne bottle." Mr Martin laughed. "Might run to lemonade though."

When the taxi pulled up outside the garage on Saturday morning, Peter and Charlie came pedalling up behind it, puffing and hot. Mrs Walters brought out a tray with a bottle of lemonade on it, a plate of cakes and a dish of lollies.

"I didn't know we were going to have a party," Charlie said. "What are we supposed to be here for? It's not my birthday."

He looked around him and seeing nothing unusual moved over to the table. Mrs Walters poured the lemonade.

"All in good time," Mr Martin told him. "Tommy's got something to show you both."

Peter pursed his mouth, picked up a glass and muttered under his breath. "It had better be good."

Tommy knew it looked as good as a new bike. Peter could say what he wanted. Now that he had a bike he was free to do anything he liked. He could ride to school, go over to the farm, down to the river and if Peter didn't want him, he'd go by himself. Everything would change. He might not even mind there being nothing around except space.

The cakes and lemonade disappeared in moments and as they munched on their "nifty bars" Tommy grew impatient.

"We'd better 'ave this 'ere launching," he said, pulling open the heavy garage door. He rushed inside and came out wheeling the bike.

"Is that yours?" Peter asked, unbelieving.

"Yeah, it's mine. It's got new paint an' everyfink."

Charlie, impressed, took hold of the handlebar, rang the bell, pressed the brake handle and tested the tyres.

"Gee Pete," he said, "it's almost as good as new."

Mr Martin stood back, looking at the boys. "Just about," he said, proud of his handiwork.

Peter moved it backwards and forwards, looking at it carefully. "Will it go?" he asked.

"Of course it'll go," Charlie said.

"One way to find out," Mr Martin told them, "give it a test run. Come on, Tommy, on you get."

They all watched him wheel it out on to the roadway, and waited while he put his foot on the pedal, swung his leg over, wobbled a bit and then rode off down the road.

Serve him right if he fell off, Peter thought. He supposed it was all right for Tommy to have a bike, but he wished his grandfather had told him about it. Anyway, it was only an old bike fixed up.

Tommy came back, ringing the bell furiously. "It's not 'arf great Mr Martin," he called. "What abaht a big ride? Down the river? Orright, Auntie?"

Charlie wanted to go and rushed off to get his bike, but Peter hung back. "Got things to do," he said, picked up his bike and rode off back along the road towards home.

His grandfather sighed, took the tray and carried it inside for Mrs Walters.

Tommy hardly noticed Peter wasn't there with them as he and Charlie rode abreast towards the turn-off for the river road. He had ridden bikes around the park in Exeter but he'd never been right out in the open road like this, with no traffic and no sounds except the caw of the crows and the occasional mooing of a cow. He rode faster and faster, the wind whistling through his hair. For a few minutes he hadn't a care in the world.

Charlie didn't notice the sound of the aircraft, but Tommy did. Faint at first, he thought it might go away, be flying in another direction, but it came straight towards them, the sound of the engines filling the air as it zoomed past them in the direction of the landing field.

He took his hands off the handlebars and clamped them over his ears. The bike wavered across the gravel road, then toppled and Tommy hurtled off into the ditch on the roadside.

Charlie pulled up and ran over to him and looked down at Tommy curled into the soft earth at the bottom of the ditch.

He scrambled down and sat quietly next to him, remembering the way Miss Leslie waited when it happened at school. He put his hand on Tommy's shoulder and after a few minutes he spoke.

"The bike's all right, Tommy," he said, "just a bit scratched."

Tommy didn't answer.

"Tommy, are you all right?" He wished he would stop shaking. "The plane's gone."

Gradually Tommy lifted his head, took his hands away from his ears and sat hunched up against the side of the ditch.

Charlie searched for something to say, not knowing whether to talk about what happened to find something else. He was curious too, so he asked softly, "What are you thinking about, Tommy? The air raids?"

"Sort of."

"Is it true a bomb fell on your house?"

"Yes."

"Were you in it?"

No answer.

"What happened?"

Tommy picked up a piece of grass and twisted it between his fingers. "We used to live in London," he said looking down into the bottom of the ditch. Not looking up. "My mam 'ated them shelters. Said they was rough."

He stopped and Charlie waited.

"So we moved away and went to Exeter and we' ad our own 'ouse and our own shelter in the backyard. . ."

Tommy's voice trailed off, his thoughts going way back to the little two storeyed house with its vegetable garden and the Anderson shelter in the back, far away from London, where his father had said they'd be safe.

"We wasn't safe. We 'eard the air-raid sirens one night and we went to our shelter an' all, and my mam read Essie and me a book and I got up to make my mam a cup of tea and. . ."

"Yes?" Charlie urged him to go on.

"I 'eard them German planes and there was a lot of noise and everyfink fell on top of me and it was black and then some men came and dug me out. Men with axes."

"What about your mum and your sister?"

Tommy didn't answer and Charlie wished he hadn't said it, but he had heard people talking about Tommy and he wanted to know. He wanted to help.

Tommy moved his legs and sat up straighter. He threw away the stalk of grass, and answered in a flat listless voice, almost talking to himself and not Charlie. "I never saw my mam and Essie any more."

Charlie waited.

"They told me about them in hospital, but I didn't believe them. My dad said we'd be safe in Exeter."

"You weren't though."

"No. A minister chap came and told me too, but I

didn't believe him. My dad wrote me a letter. He were in Africa and they wouldn't let him come back. He said it really were true.''

"Did you want to come to Australia?''

"I didn't care. My dad wrote that there'd be sun and no bombs so I fort it'd be all right. 'E said there'd be no war, but 'e didn't say nothink about the planes.''

"They're transports, those planes,'' Charlie told him, "they're not bombers or anything.''

"Sound the same.'' Tommy began pushing himself to his feet. He stood up and reached out to his bike.

"It's just got a few scratches, that's all,'' Charlie reassured him. "Mr Martin can fix them up.''

They examined the bike together and Charlie asked, "Do you think you should go and live somewhere else. Somewhere where there aren't any planes?''

"What you say that for?''

"Just wondered.''

"I don't want to go nowhere else,'' Tommy answered. "I like me auntie.''

"Then you've got to get better. Golly, Tommy, isn't there any way you can stop getting scared of the planes?''

"I dunno. I try. But I 'ear the noise and I see everyfink 'appen all over and I can't stop.''

"Well, I'm going to find a way,'' Charlie said picking up his bike and standing next to Tommy. "Let's ride down to the river and while we're there I'll think of something.'' He got on to his bike. "I'll think of something if it's the last thing I do.''

His mind churned over the problem as they rode along the river bank on the rough track. He stopped beside a big old weeping willow tree, put his bike down and leaned against the trunk. Tommy stood near him watching the river run past, brown and muddy with occasional swirls where the water hit the banks.

"The whole trouble is," Charlie said, thinking as he spoke each word, "the noise. So—how can we stop the noise?"

"Can't," Tommy replied.

"Yes we can. I've read about it. A sound-proof room, that's what we need."

"I can't stay in a sound-proof room all me life," Tommy exploded.

Charlie went on, not listening to Tommy. "We can put stuff all around the classroom, that'll make it sound-proof and then you wouldn't hear the planes."

"Charlie! 'Ow could we do that? What about the winders? And anyway, what about when I went 'ome?"

Charlie thought again. "No, we couldn't do that." His eyes opened wide as his thoughts raced around his head.

"I know. You've got to stop hearing the noise, right?"

Tommy nodded, but wasn't expecting Charlie to say anything really possible. He was right.

"Instead of making the rooms sound-proof, we could make your ears sound-proof. Put cotton wool in them and you wouldn't hear the planes."

"I wouldn't 'ear nuffin' else, neither," Tommy told him. "I couldn't do me lessons or listen to the wireless or 'ear you say all them nutty things you're saying now." He ran along the path to the next tree and called back. "Maybe that's not such a bad idea."

"It's a start though," Charlie called back and squeezed his eyes almost shut as he thought about it.

"What about the night time? I 'ear them inside me 'ead then, even when they're not there."

"You didn't tell me about that," Charlie said.

Suddenly the whole day had become cold and bleak. They decided to ride back home.

7   ALFREDO

The next afternoon, Sunday, Charlie's mother asked him to ride up to the farm and give Mrs Turner a message, so he called in for Peter on the way.

"We're going to have a party for Tim," Charlie told him. "He's got his call-up."

As they wheeled their bikes out on to the roadway, Charlie, hesitating, said to Peter, "Will we ask Tommy to come?"

"To the party?"

"No. You know what I mean—up to the farm with us."

Peter busied himself twisting the pedal of his bike.

Charlie waited for him to reply, and added, "It's true about his mum and sister."

"How do you know?"

"I asked him."

"That doesn't mean it's true."

"A bomb fell on his house."

Peter went on fixing the pedal.

"You wouldn't like it," Charlie said, getting angry.

Peter gave the pedal a few twists, then got on to the bike.

"You could try being nice to him," Charlie said.

"It was better before he came here. He doesn't have to tag along with us all the time."

"It doesn't hurt."

Peter rode off but turned back when Charlie didn't follow. "I suppose we'll ask him then," he said and they rode around the corner into Tommy's street.

As they slid their bikes to a halt, Tommy stopped playing with his ball and walked over to them, surprised to see Peter. But Peter or not, he wanted to go up to the farm. He told his aunt where he was going and wheeled his bike out of the garage. No one spoke about the two big scratches down the mudguard. They turned off on to the dirt road leading to the farm and rode three abreast.

"Miss Leslie's coming to see me auntie," Tommy announced as they rode.

"What for?" Peter asked.

"To talk about me," Tommy said. "She always wants to talk about me. I don't want to be there."

"Well, you're not," Charlie said brightly. "We'll stay out till she's gone."

Feeling sure that there was now no chance of his meeting up with Miss Leslie, Tommy breathed in deeply and pedalled fast into the wind.

Peter opened the farm gates and they rode up the long tree-lined drive to the farmyard, scattering the fowls and ducks. They left their bikes near the hand pump at the kitchen door, and called a greeting.

Usually things were very quiet on the farm on Sunday afternoons, but today Mrs Turner hardly turned around as they came to the door. There was a smell of cakes cooking, a pile of fresh apples on the bench and masses of freshly made butter.

"Have you heard our news?" she called.

"No," Charlie answered, walking through the doorway, "Mum sent me round to tell you our news. Tim's got his call-up papers. He's going to Sydney next week-end and we're going to have a party. Mum says, can you come?"

"Tim!" she exclaimed. "Well, he'll be going off just as our Bill arrives home on leave." She nodded her head as she spoke. "After nearly two and a half years. Back home."

Bob Turner came up behind them. "It's only leave, Mother. They'll be sending him to New Guinea just as soon as they can."

The boys, standing in the kitchen, saw a flash of sadness cross her face as she plunged a knife into a peeled apple.

"But it's not as far away as Africa," she said, "not half as far."

"Why's 'e coming 'ome, Mr Turner?" Tommy looked worried. "Is the war over in Africa?"

"Far from it." Mr Turner sat down, picked up a piece of apple and began to chew it. "We need our men here. Churchill doesn't want to send them back, but this is where they should be. No use to us in Africa."

"My dad's in Africa."

"Well, Tommy, I'm afraid there's still a lot of fighting to be done there. But the Aussies have done their bit. The Japs are the ones we've got to worry about now."

"Do you think they'll invade us, Mr Turner?" Charlie asked, a ring of excitement in his voice. "Where do you think they'll land? My auntie's going to leave Sydney and go and live in the mountains."

"We haven't got so much to worry about now that Bill's coming home." Smiling, Mr Turner offered the boys an apple each. "He and his mates'll send them packing."

"I could go up there if they'd let me," Peter said. "Bet I could shoot a gun."

Mrs Turner picked up a large saucepan and moved it on to the stove. "Whoever heard of such a thing." She bent down and stirred up the fire vigorously. "Now you boys go off and have a good search for eggs. I'm going to need as many as I can get.''

''What about the party?'' Charlie asked, disappointed that nobody seemed to be as excited as he was.

She wiped her hands on a small towel and walked over to the telephone on the kitchen wall. ''What do you think, Bob? What if we have a party too— combine one for Bill with one for Tim?'' She didn't wait for an answer but lifted the receiver. ''I'll ring your mother, Charlie, and see what she thinks.'' She waited for the operator to answer. ''What about it, Bob? One big party for them both?''

''Will there be twice as much to eat?'' Charlie asked. ''If there is I think it's a great idea.''

''There'll be enough, you can be sure of that,'' Mr Turner said and strode out into the yard. ''Leave the arrangements to the women. Have a good look for eggs, then you can go down to the river if you want to. Jo and Alfredo are looking for heifers. Might be a few down there.''

Tommy wondered who Jo and Alfredo were. Alfredo seemed a funny sort of name. Alf maybe, or Fred, for Alfredo? They must be the men he saw doing the milking.

The hens laid their eggs all over the farmyard. Under the bushes, in the shed, in little scooped out holes near the sides of the buildings. They found ten and took them into the kitchen, then they went through the dairy, out the gate and across the paddock to the river.

''Who's Jo and Alfredo?'' Tommy asked as they walked.

''You know, you saw them last time.''

''The ones that was milkin'? What's 'e called Alfredo for?''

'''Cause that's his name, he's an Italian,'' Peter answered. ''A prisoner-of-war.''

Tommy stared in disbelief. "A prisoner-of-war!" Peter was making it up. "Don't believe ya."

"He's been here for months. Both have," Peter told him nonchantly. "My grandad said it's better having them doing work on farms and places than just sitting about doing nothing. Uncle Bob's got to pay them and everything."

Tommy still found it hard to understand.

"Where were they, then, when they were captured?" he asked.

"North Africa. There were thousands of Italians taken prisoner there. They took Alfredo to India first then they sent some to England, some to Canada and some here."

"But won't they escape?" Tommy asked.

"Grandad says there's nowhere they can go. They haven't got any identity cards and they can't speak English much. Anyway they don't mind being here."

Charlie joined in. "Alfredo does sometimes. He wants to go back to his family."

"Well he can't," Peter said with finality. "He's got to stay here. They both have to."

Tommy had never thought that there'd be actual prisoners walking about and working on farms, and by the time it had all sunk into his head they'd reached the river.

They found Alfredo and Jo on the bank under the low branches of a willow tree, trying to coax a frightened heifer out into the open and away from the treacherous, soft mud on the banks. They worked hard pushing and prodding and at last the animal took a great leap and bounded off up into the paddock.

The two men laughed and rubbed their muddy hands against their trouser legs, then walked up to the boys.

"How many have you found?" Peter asked.

"Eh?" the shorter of the two men called.

"How many?" Peter repeated.

The man held up three fingers. "Three."

"This is Tommy, Alfredo," Charlie said to the smaller dark-haired man with the wide, friendly smile. "And this is Jo, Tommy."

The other man was taller, thinner and younger and didn't seem so friendly. "My name is Giovanni," he said.

"We can't say that," Charlie told Tommy, "so we say Jo."

The men walked ahead and they all followed up into the paddock.

They talked as they walked, Charlie doing most of the explaining. Alfredo understood a little English and could answer, but it seemed difficult for him. When Charlie told him that Tommy had come out from England he showed a lot of interest.

"A ship?" he asked.

"Yes," Tommy told him, "in a convoy." Then he realised Alfredo wouldn't understand. "A lot of ships togever."

"*Si*," Alfredo said eagerly. "Me too, I came in shipa."

Tommy picked up a stick and drew on a pitch of bare ground. He drew six ships and then around them, almost in a circle, he drew four more with guns pointing outwards. "Destroyers," he said, "to keep off the submarines."

"Submarines?" Alfredo repeated. "You see submarines?"

"No, we didn't see none but we might 'ave. We 'ad to be careful." And realising that Alfredo could not understand much of what he said he spoke to Charlie and Peter.

"We couldn't 'ardly make any noise in case they 'eard us and we couldn't drop nothing overboard, not even a lolly paper or a match 'cos if they found it they'd know we was there and come after us. And at night we had to blackout every bit of light. Cigarettes even.''

Tommy thought back to the weeks he had spent on the ship, remembering the lifesaving drill every day. They had all been told exactly where they had to assemble to get into a lifeboat and where to find their lifejackets and how to put them on. At first they'd run all over the deck looking for their stations, but in a few days they'd all known exactly where to go and did what they were told as quickly as they could. Sometimes he'd stood at the ship's rail with the other children, and looked at the escorting destroyers in the distance and wondered just whereabouts in that huge ocean the enemy submarines really were.

''Which way you come?'' Alfredo asked, very serious.

''In a ship,'' Tommy said. ''I told you that.''

Charlie broke in. ''He means which way. Which countries?''

Tommy told him as clearly as he could that they had left Tilbury in England and gone south past Spain to the African coast, then stopped for a while in Durban in South Africa, then right across the Indian Ocean to Perth in Australia. After that they'd gone round the south of Australia to Adelaide, Melbourne and then Sydney.

''You have a mappa?'' Alfredo asked.

The three boys looked at one another, each wondering what Alfredo meant.

''I wonder what sort of map he means,'' Peter said.

''We've got an atlas,'' Charlie announced. ''That'll show you.''

''Bring me the mappa,'' Alfredo demanded.

''Okay, if you want us to,'' Charlie said, not quite sure of Alfredo's sudden change of mood.

Jo walked on. He didn't seem interested in the talk about the map.

On their way home the boys talked about the Italians and why Alfredo was so interested in the map.

"Where do they sleep?" Tommy asked, wondering whether they were locked in at night or went off to some barracks.

"They've got beds in the barn," Peter answered. "Aunt Hannah takes their meals to them. She lets them cook their own food on Saturday afternoons. I've been there sometimes. It smells good."

"What do you fink he wanted the map for?" Tommy asked.

"Dunno. Maybe just wants to know where the places are. Just interested. I dunno."

"Will we take it?" Charlie asked.

Peter shrugged. "Grandad said he couldn't run far even if he wanted to. If we take up an atlas at least he can see where all the places you talked about are."

"And where Italy is," Tommy added.

"He'd never get there from here, even if he wanted to." Peter was quite sure about that. "It's thousands of miles away."

"So's England," Tommy said, "and Africa."

Charlie rode out in front. "I don't know what you're both talking about," he called over his shoulder. "We're going to need our atlases anyway. We've got to find out where Flinders went, for homework, and it's got to be ready by tomorrow. Come on."

"Now you've gone and reminded me about Miss Leslie." Tommy suddenly felt dejected. "I'm not going inside if she's still there."

He used to think she was the nicest teacher he'd ever known. But now he wasn't so sure. He wished she'd stop trying to tell his auntie what to do.

They rode slowly past the shop to the corner of the road and tried to peer through the windows as they rode. Tommy really couldn't tell if Miss Leslie had left or not, so he asked Charlie and Peter to wait while he went quietly to the door and listened. All he could hear was his aunt singing a song to herself, so he waved the others off and went inside.

He didn't want his aunt to talk about Miss Leslie, so he quickly started to talk himself. "Auntie, did you know Mr Turner, the farmer Mr Turner, 'as two prisoners-of-war on 'is farm? Italians."

"Yes, I knew. Everybody does. I thought he would have told you about them when you went up before."

"No. I saw 'em though, but no one said nuffin' about 'em then."

"Hannah Turner quite likes them. They work hard. . . Miss Leslie's just gone."

He ignored that piece of information. "Mrs Turner's goin' to 'ave a party because 'er son Bill's coming 'ome and Tim's going away."

"Bill's coming home! Ooh, that's good news." She put two cups and saucers away. "Miss Leslie's very concerned about you."

"And that Peter wasn't 'arf bad today."

"She's worried about you, Tommy."

"She wants me to talk posh."

"That's not what she came about. She's pleased with your work at school."

"What'd you talk about then?"

"She did all the talking. I told her you were getting along just fine. Got your bike an' all. Going out with the boys. Nothing to worry about."

"Then what's she worrying for?" he asked.

"You know, luv, it's the planes."

"Carn' 'elp it. Got to do me 'omework now." He stood up and rushed down the hall to his bedroom.

"You go along then, luv," his aunt called. "Tea'll be ready soon."

He took out his exercise book and atlas and put them

on the table in front of him, opened the atlas and turned to the map of Africa. He found Libya and gazed out of the window thinking about the miles and miles between him and his father. It grew dark and he forgot to turn on the light. In a little while his aunt called him for his tea so he closed the atlas and walked back into the kitchen.

8   ONE BIG PARTY

Charlie sat on the end of Tim's bed and watched his brother sort through his wardrobe. The pile of things beside him grew as Tim discarded books, pencils, games and clothes and handed them over to Charlie.

Tim didn't need to take very much with him—he had been sent a list. But he wanted to leave his room spic and span as he knew he would only be coming back to it during the odd periods of leave. It might be years before he'd live in it again, and in the Navy he wouldn't have much room for possessions, especially if he were on a ship.

He'd read everything he could find about Navy life and now he wondered how he could possibly wait, even for the few days left. After reporting to Woolloomooloo he'd be sent down to Flinders for training, but he didn't know what would happen after that. He'd be sent somewhere. A ship? Land base? He didn't know. He just hoped it would be a ship.

He and Charlie had been making a model aeroplane to give to Peter for his birthday and finishing that would be one way to fill in the time. Then there was the party.

Bill Turner had arrived home the day before and, going by the number of people who had been invited up to the farm that night, the walls would be bulging.

"What do you do at parties?" Charlie asked, "grown-up parties?"

"Dance a bit," Tim replied, standing back and looking at his cupboard with everything hanging or stacked neat and tidy. "There'll be music, they've got a piano and a gramophone."

"I don't want to listen to music. I can do that here." Charlie didn't feel enthusiastic.

"You can eat then. That'll keep you occupied."

Charlie brightened. "Well, that's something. I'll start at one end of the table and work my way down to the end."

"How's your mate, Tommy?" Tim asked. "Where are they going to send him? Do you know?"

Charlie looked up quickly. "What do you mean, send him? He's here."

"Heard Mum talking. Didn't you know? Your school-teacher wants him to go away from Tiboorie."

Charlie jumped off the bed and scooped the pile of things into his arms. "I didn't know that." Holding his pile of new belongings, he half ran into his room and dumped them on his bed. Then he came back. "Are you sure?"

"No, not really. I just heard Mum talking on the phone. Don't get into a panic."

"I'm not. I just didn't know." And he turned and ran out the front door. "Tell Mum, I'll be back in a while. I've got to see Peter."

"Don't be late. You've got to have a bath and get dressed."

Charlie waved behind him, dismissing even the prospect of washing himself before going out, and raced off to Peter's.

They sat together on the edge of the veranda, their legs dangling into the garden.

"What's Miss Leslie got to do with it?" Peter asked. "Mrs Walters's his auntie."

"Do you want him to go? You said you did before."

"Well," Peter hesitated, "I don't know. He isn't as bad as I thought. He's pretty bad, but not that bad."

"I know he doesn't want to go anywhere else."

"Of course he doesn't. Anyway, where would he go? They can't send him back to England."

The two sat looking down into the garden, knocking the tops off the flowers with their feet.

"I've been trying to think up a way to get him to stop his shakes," Charlie said.

"Why?"

"Why do you think?" Charlie answered. "I feel sorry, that's why, and anyway I bet Mrs Walters wouldn't want him to go anywhere. She'd be all by herself again if he went." Charlie scratched the side of his face thoughtfully. "And we wouldn't get any more free lollies."

"What do you want to do?" Peter asked, "stop the aeroplanes?"

"That's an idea." Charlie looked up, his eyes bright with interest. "You could ask your dad to get all the planes that fly over this side of town to fly in and out on the other side." He grinned with satisfaction. "I knew we'd think of something."

"I'll ask my dad," Peter spoke each word slowly and carefully, "to write a letter to General Macarthur and say, 'Dear General Macarthur, please don't fly your planes over Tiboorie school because we have a kid here called Tommy Hooper and he doesn't like them. Don't worry about the war'."

"Well, you could try."

Peter swung himself down from the veranda and jumped across the garden bed to the lawn. "And pigs could fly!'' he said. "Anyway, I've got to go in. Mum wants us to leave at 7.30.''

Charlie walked home slowly, and dressed himself for the party. When Jack Martin arrived it was his second trip up to the farm. He had taken Mr and Mrs Andrews, Pam and Peter on the first trip and came back for Mrs Calder, Tim and Charlie, and Mrs Walters and Tommy.

"I won't be able to do anything with this tie on,'' Charlie muttered as they neared the farm house. "I feel as though I'm in a strait-jacket.''

"You look very nice,'' Mrs Walters told him, "and so does Tommy. You've got to get dressed up for a party, Charlie. That's part of it all.''

"But you and Mum haven't got ties on.'' He looked at them both closely and added, half to himself, "You haven't even got sleeves in your dresses.''

They heard the music as they passed through the driveway gates, but, with all the windows and doors covered by blackout curtains, the whole house appeared to be in darkness. Mr Martin stopped the taxi at the front door and they all slipped through the curtains into the bright lights of the party.

About twenty people stood around the room. Mrs Turner sat at the piano thumping out a tune, men and women talked in groups, most of them holding glasses and as Tommy and his aunt looked around them a tall man in khaki uniform came up to them.

Tommy had never seen an Australian army uniform before and he thought how much cooler and simpler it was than the British uniform his father wore.

It was Bill Turner. Tommy shook hands with him, then raced off to find Charlie. He found him talking to some of the girls from their class at school and left them as soon as he could and went across to Jack Martin and his aunt.

"Enjoying yourself?" Jack Martin asked.

"I fort Alfredo and Jo'd be here," Tommy said. At the mention of the two names Mr Martin looked around him and seeing no one in hearing distance bent down a little and said quietly. "Better not mention them tonight, lad. Been a bit of a row, I think."

"What happened?" Mrs Walters asked, her eyebrows raised.

"You can understand how Bill felt. He came back home, been fighting the Italians and Germans in Libya and he finds two Italians here on his father's farm. He reckons they get treated better than our men in the army. He's pretty cranky."

Before Tommy had time to think any more about it, Mrs Turner stopped playing, and called across to Mrs Walters. They'd start the dancing with the Lambeth Walk. Mrs Walters took charge.

"Come on now, I'll show you all how to do it," she put out her arms and beckoned everyone to come into the centre of the room. "Line up, take a partner. Where's a partner for me? Come on Tommy, luv. You can do it. Everyone from London can do the Lambeth Walk."

It went on for ages, everyone clapping at the end of the chorus, wanting it again and again and, by the time Mrs Turner pealed out the last notes, the whole gathering was shouting out the words and weaving in and out to the music. Even Charlie and Peter danced, partnered by two of the girls from school and across the room Tommy saw Bill Turner with his arm held tightly around Miss Leslie's waist.

But he felt hot and slipped away from his aunt's side, took a glass of orange juice and sat on a chair by the window.

Alfredo and Jo would be down in the barn listening, he thought. They wouldn't be asleep, there was too much noise, so he put his glass down and slipped past the blackout curtain through the open door.

The farmyard in front of him was quiet and dark. No hens scuttled about, no dogs, no ducks. They must have been safely and securely asleep somewhere. He saw the shape of the barn outlined against the brightness of the night and thought he could see the shape of someone sitting outside. He called out as he neared the door.

Alfredo answered. "Tommy, I see you coming."

"I 'aven't got the map. I'll bring it next time," Tommy said and Alfredo moved two boxes next to the wall and sat down on one. Tommy sat on the other.

"It is a good party?"

Tommy nodded. "Very good."

"Today I am—*triste*."

Tommy looked up questioningly.

"Er, I am...I am sad."

"You want to go to the party?"

"No." Alfredo narrowed his eyes. "I no want to go to the party. I sad for my family. *Si*. In Salerno. My mamma, my papa, my sisters, my wife."

"Do you get letters?" Tommy asked, thinking about the letters he received each week from his father.

"I no get letters. But soon they come. Mr Turner told me."

Tommy knew that Alfredo understood some English, but was not sure how much. He spoke carefully and slowly. "My dad's in Libya. Was you there?"

"*Si*. My *unita* was in Libya. A very bad war. *Brutta*." He spread out his hands and raised his shoulders.

"Guns and sand. We not know what happens. And then we...*catturati*."

"Captured?" Tommy volunteered.

"*Si*. We go to India. Then we go to Australia."

"In a ship."

"*Si*. Like you. Now my family is very far." He stayed quiet for a long time, then he said. "I must return."

"You carn' do that," Tommy said quickly. "You 'aven't got any papers and you carn't talk English properly." He had forgotten about speaking slowly in his surprise. "Mr Martin said you wouldn't get far if you did try."

"You help?"

Tommy leaned back against the wall and breathed out hard. Of course Alfredo would want to go home. He understood how much he must be missing his family, but apart from Bill getting cranky about his being there, no one was hurting him. At least he was away from the war.

His aunt called from the veranda of the farmhouse. "Tommy, are you out there? Tommy!"

He jumped off the box and straightened his coat and tie. "I 'ave to go, Alfredo."

Alfredo thrust out his hand and grabbed Tommy by the arm. "You help, Tommy?" he repeated, his eyes narrow and piercing.

"I'll bring the atlas next week," he said, twisting away from Alfredo's grasp and racing across the yard to the veranda.

"I've been looking for you everywhere," Mrs Walters said. "Wherever've you been? I've been fair worried out of my mind."

"Just looking at the chickens," he said. "They was asleep."

"Supper's ready. The party's inside, not outside. Come on now."

And the two pulled back the blackout curtains and went back into the living room.

Charlie had already started on his campaign of eating and was about a quarter way down the table. Peter sat with Tim and Pam, holding a plate stacked with sausage rolls and cakes and Tommy noticed Miss Leslie standing very close to Bill as they waited to go to the supper table.

With the table almost empty and people sitting holding their glasses, Jack Martin rose to his feet and made a speech, welcoming Bill home from the war in North Africa, wishing him well for his next period of action in New Guinea and giving Tim everyone's best wishes and prayers for his safety in the Navy. It was a solemn speech.

Tommy saw the tears in Mrs Calder's eyes and saw Pam, holding Tim's hand, squeeze it hard. And he thought about Alfredo sitting under the stars outside the wooden barn, thousands of miles away from his own family in Salerno. He thought of his father in Africa and wondered what he would be doing at that very moment. He saw tanks pushing their way through the desert sands, heard guns firing, crashed planes burning. He felt the heat and the windblown sand and he blinked hard so that it would go away. But he kept seeing his father, gun in hand, shooting across the desert at the enemy and Alfredo, sweating in the hot desert, shooting back.

9   FORWARD PLANNING

Tommy would have taken the atlas to Alfredo earlier if it hadn't been for Bill. He had had it with him on two occasions when he visited the farm, but each time Bill was there and he couldn't get to Alfredo by himself.

As he walked past him Alfredo asked, but Tommy just shook his head.

Before lunch one Saturday Charlie called in to see him. They sat on the steps of the shop in the still air, blue cloudless sky and warm sun. It was a perfect autumn day.

"Guess who's gone for a picnic?" Charlie asked Tommy.

"'Arf of Tiboorie, I'd reckon," Tommy replied.

Charlie leaned back, pleased with himself because he knew something Tommy didn't. "Miss Leslie."

"Nuffink to do wiv me," Tommy said, disappointed with Charlie's big secret.

"But," Charlie cocked his head sideways, "she's gone with Bill Turner. I saw them walking down the river road with a basket."

"Well, the only good thing about that is," Tommy said, "is. . .it'll keep Miss Leslie out of the way for—"

He stopped suddenly. "Cor, it'll keep 'im out o' the way too. We can go up and see Alfredo." He stood up. "An' take the map." He shook Charlie's shoulder. "Come on."

"I haven't had my lunch yet," Charlie moved his hand in the direction of his home.

"Don't matter about lunch."

"Yes it does. Mum'll be by herself. I'll have lunch and come back."

"Don't take long then. I'll get me atlas and meet you outside in 'arf an 'our."

Charlie got on to his bike but Tommy ran after him.

"What about Peter?" he shouted.

"He's playing football with his grandad," Charlie yelled, still riding.

"Hey, Charlie." Tommy cupped his hands around his mouth as he called.

Charlie pedalled his bike into the centre of the road and then wheeled around and came back.

"Don't tell no one what we're doin'," Tommy warned as he stopped beside him.

"I'm not stupid," said Charlie and turned back along the road towards home.

The smells coming from the farm kitchen as they approached it were very different from the usual ones. They looked in through the window and saw Jo chopping up tomatoes on the kitchen table and Alfredo stirring a large saucepan on the stove.

"Easy to see Bill's not here," Charlie said and they walked in through the open door.

Jo looked up in surprise and Alfredo beamed at them with pleasure, especially when he saw that Tommy was carrying a square, thin parcel.

Making sure no one else was around, Tommy put the parcel on the table and carefully opened it. He turned to the map of the world on the first page.

Alfredo gave a quick stir to the pot and then came across to the table. Jo slowed his chopping and looked down at the book. Charlie, Tommy and Alfredo huddled around it.

"That's where we are," Charlie said, then traced his finger half way across the page. "And there's Italy."

Alfredo rubbed his chin. "A lot of sea. I think of it."

"You'll have to think for an awful long time to find a way to get from 'ere to there," Tommy told him. "Even if you did, it'd take so long the war'd be over."

"My family need me. They have no man."

He reached for his shirt pocket and took out a leather folder, and from it he pulled out a small photograph and handed it to Tommy. He and Charlie found themselves looking at a picture of a young, dark-haired woman standing beside an old stone wall.

"My wife," Alfredo told them with pride and pleasure.

"She looks nice," Tommy told him and Charlie added, "Yes, she's pretty."

"Have you got any children?" Charlie asked.

"No. We marry when my wife write on the paper in Italy and I write on the paper in Africa. We marry."

"You mean to say," Charlie asked wanting to understand just what Alfredo had said. "You got married when you both weren't there?"

"I was there," Alfredo told him firmly. "Now I go home. We marry in a churcha."

"Never heard of anyone doing it like that before," Charlie muttered, but Alfredo went on. "I find shipa. See, I go here."

They all studied the map carefully and Alfredo put the photo back into his pocket.

"I didn't know Italy was so close to Africa," Tommy said. "Look." He pointed to Libya. "That's where my dad is. Cor lumme, it's a long way from 'ere."

Charlie drew his finger along the Red Sea up to the Suez Canal. "My grandma went on a ship right through the Suez Canal. There. See. Sent me a photo of her on a camel next to the pyramids. I'd like to go there."

"Not now you wouldn't," Tommy told him.

Alfredo closed the atlas and wrapped it again in the paper. "I keep it?" he asked.

"Not for long," Tommy told him. "I've got to 'ave it at school."

"Please come Monday. But no say anything."

They looked at him and saw the cold, dark expression in his eyes again. Jo stopped chopping and held the knife high above the board as he waited for them to answer.

Both boys gulped. "No, we won't say anything," they blurted out.

Then Tommy added. "Of course we won't, Alfredo. We wouldn't 'ave brought the map if we was goin' to do that."

The two men relaxed. Alfredo put the parcel under some brown paper bags and went back to the stove. "You want eat our pasta?" he asked them. "Spaghetti?"

Tommy looked into the pot and watched while Joe scooped the tomatoes into the bubbling meat. Alfredo put on a saucepan of water and began grating a large piece of cheese. Before long they had put out four plates and forks and served the steaming spaghetti, covered with rich meaty sauce.

"A bit o' all right, this," Tommy said, moving it with his fork. "Ours used to come in tins."

Alfredo laughed loudly and Jo smiled.

"The English know nothing about cooking."

"Yes they does," Tommy said bristling.

"Nothing of food. Come eat."

Charlie sucked the long strands of spaghetti up into his mouth. "Just as well I didn't have much for lunch," he said, "I like this."

They ate together, then the two boys helped Alfredo and Jo tidy the kitchen and carry their things back to their sleeping quarters in the barn.

Before they left Alfredo said to them, "First I think a plan, then you help. Okay?"

"I don't suppose it'd make much difference to the war if you did get back to Italy," Charlie said, "but I don't think you'll be able to."

"I want see my wife. I no want fight," Alfredo said seriously.

"What about Jo?"

Alfredo dismissed the question with a curt look at his companion. "He want stay."

They left the two putting their things away before getting ready for the milking. Bill would be back soon, they knew, and they didn't want to be seen with the Italians in the barn, so they left, promising to come on Monday to collect the atlas from behind the hen's nest under the water tank. They hurried through the farmyard and sped off down the driveway, not wanting to see Bill or Mr and Mrs Turner. They just might be looking a bit too excited and someone could begin asking questions.

"Do you think we'd get into trouble if we were found out?" Charlie asked as they rode along together.

"Course we would, but we 'aven't done nuffink yet. Only lent 'im an old atlas."

"Are we going to do anything else?"

Tommy shrugged his shoulders. "If you was in Italy and wanted to go back to Australia, you'd want someone to 'elp you, wouldn't you? Your dad'd want someone to 'elp 'im get back 'ome. You'd want someone to do that."

"Yes, I suppose I would. But Alfredo's an enemy."

"Not a real one," Tommy answered quickly, "not like the Germans. He don't want to fight no one. He just wants to go 'ome."

Charlie wasn't so sure. "He's a prisoner-of-war though."

"So's your dad."

"We don't know that."

"You fink 'e is. That's good enough."

Charlie thought for a moment about his father somewhere in Malaya, in the jungle or in a prison camp and how he would be missing them all, thinking about them. And how he'd be wanting to get back. "What do you think Alfredo'll ask us to do?" he asked.

"We'll 'ave to wait and see. An' don't say a word to no one. Not no one."

"Peter?"

"We'll 'ave to tell 'im. He knows most of it anyway. But not a person else. Or we'll end up being an 'orrible sight."

Tommy went by himself to collect his atlas on Monday afternoon. The first thing he did at the farm was to find some eggs and put them on the special shelf in the farm kitchen. Then he picked up the parcel under the tank stand and just as he was about to speed off home, Bill came along and started to talk. Tommy, with the parcel tucked into his shirt, tried not to look worried. They were used to him coming up to the farm now, collecting hen eggs and pottering about. Mr Turner had told him to come and visit any time he liked.

Bill leaned against the fence and asked Tommy how he was getting on, talked about his father in Africa and how he had fought there too, but mostly he talked about how

Tommy liked being in Tiboorie. So much so that next day Tommy asked Charlie about it.

"Why does Bill keep asking me if I like being 'ere?'' he said to Charlie as they walked home from school.

"Well, do you?" Charlie asked.

"What's everyone want to know that for, then?"

Peter caught up with them and they all walked together.

"You've been a bit better though, with the aeroplanes," Charlie said.

"Miss Leslie doesn't think so," Peter remarked.

"What you on about?" Tommy felt annoyed. "'Ow do you know what she finks?"

"She asked my dad," Peter replied, "and he said, because I heard them talking on the phone, that there's masses of Americans coming now we've won the Coral Sea battle and there'll be more aeroplanes."

"And we're still trying to think of a way to get you to stop that shaking thing," Charlie told him. He turned to Peter. "Did you ask your Dad about stopping the planes coming over like we said?"

"Of course I didn't. Anyway Grandad says you've got to face up to the things that frighten you."

Tommy kicked a stone angrily. "'Ow can I face an aeroplane? They're in the sky."

"Some of them aren't," Charlie said, "some of them are on the ground. I know. . ." He stopped still. "I know what we could do. We could go out to the aerodrome every day until you get used to them."

Neither Tommy nor Peter answered him.

"Well, it's an idea," he said.

"Pretty silly one," Peter rejoined. "Like going into a lion's den."

They reached the corner and Peter and Charlie went one way, Tommy the other.

As they ate their meal that night, Tommy asked his aunt about the way Bill talked to him. "He's real friendly with my school-teacher," he said, "and the way he talked you'd fink she was goin' to try and send me somewheres. I fort she liked me."

"Oh, she's just hot air," his aunt replied, "a lot of talk."

"No it's not, Auntie. She talked to everyone."

"Well, talkin's not doin'."

"She can't do nuffin anyway. You're me auntie."

"She can talk to the Child Welfare, luv. They're keeping an eye on you. Keeping an eye on all the children evacuated out here. Even if they do live with their aunties."

"You mean she can ask them to send me somewhere even if you don't want them to?"

"She could try." Mrs Walters sat straight in her chair and held her lips tightly together. "But I don't like her chances." She plunged her fork into her meat and cut vigorously. "Seems to me there's a lot of people saying things round here. It might be time for Marion Walters to start saying something."

Tommy smiled. "One thing I do know," he said.

"What's that?" she asked, still cutting furiously.

"We'll be safe from the Japs if they come. They'll just take one look at you and run."

She gave a brief smile, then looked serious again. "I've got me mettle up now," she said. "You're staying here with me and I'm the one that's looking after you. I'm the one who'll do the worrying."

Tommy started eating, feeling secure in his aunt's anger. He was getting used to being at Tiboorie. He had Alfredo and Jo to think about and he had his bike. He settled back knowing that if Miss Leslie wanted to move him away, she'd have to fight Marion Walters first.

10   FRIENDS AND ENEMIES

Tim came home on leave for a few days after leaving Flinders and before going to Garden Island. On the first day he walked proudly down the main road wearing his brand new uniform, his belt and gaiters shining white and his boots shining black, his jacket tight and his pants flaring.

Charlie followed him wherever he went, and tried on his cap whenever Tim would let him. Even though Tim was his brother he certainly looked as good to Charlie as any sailor he had ever seen. Not that he had seen many, but once, when he had visited Sydney he'd seen lots of men from all the armed forces. American, British, but he had liked the Australian sailor's uniform best.

Garden Island was the big naval depot in Sydney Harbour. Tim knew that he and his mates wouldn't be there for very long—they would be posted to either a land base somewhere in Australia, or a ship. They all hoped against hope it would be a ship, but in the meantime all Tim told them was that he would be sleeping on HMAS *Kuttabul*. He rather slid over the fact that it was an old Sydney ferry boat fitted out for sleeping quarters, but at least it was on the water.

Mrs Calder invited some friends in for supper the night before Tim left, but even Tommy could see that Tim wished they would all go home and he could be alone with Pam.

Bill came, and spent most of the night sitting next to Miss Leslie. His leave was up in a few days' time. When he reported back to his unit, they would all go north to New Guinea. He dodged the questions everyone asked and would only say that they would probably go north by train, then by ship from one of the northern ports to New Guinea.

Anyway, he explained, even if he did know he wouldn't tell them. Everyone understood. Notices appeared on every wall from the railway station to the town hall, saying, THE ENEMY IS LISTENING. No one talked, but everyone knew that troops were moving north as rapidly as possible.

A few days after Tim's departure, Bill and three other soldiers from the district were due to catch the train at Tiboorie station. Miss Leslie took the whole class down there to see them off. Some members of the local band came, the children waved flags, the band played marching tunes and as Bill stepped on to the train, Miss Leslie put out her hand to him. Taking no notice of the people watching, he bent down, put his arm around her and kissed her. The children cheered and waved their flags and to the tune of "Wish me Luck as you Wave me Goodbye", the train slowly moved off.

To Tommy everything seemed unreal. The little railway station with just a few soldiers leaving, was so different from the ranks of soldiers he had seen on the London railway station the time his father had gone back from leave. And the enemy Bill was going off to fight was the Japanese, not the Germans. He had known about the Germans for as long as he could remember. He could hardly think back to the time when there had been no war, when there hadn't been soldiers and sailors and airmen on the streets in uniform, and anti-aircraft guns and sandbags and blackouts and big notices pointing to the air-raid shelters.

Once a week Mrs Walters and Tommy went to the picture theatre. Newsreel pictures were shown before the main film started, mostly about battles in various areas of the world, and when they showed anything about the African campaigns Tommy strained forward, looking hard in case one of the soldiers just happened to be his father.

It didn't seem a real war here in Tiboorie. It was all so far away.

He found it hard to think of Alfredo and Jo being prisoners-of-war. They seemed just like anyone else, working and sleeping, talking and laughing. Missing their families.

"I wouldn't 'elp 'em if they was Germans," Tommy said as they walked down to the dairy a few days later.

"No one said we were going to help them," Peter reminded him. "We're just going to listen to what they have to say."

Mr Turner had had the milking machines installed and they found Alfredo and Jo absorbed in their task of fixing the machines to the cows' teats, seeing that the milk ran smoothly through the tubes to the big steel container and soothing the cows.

Mr Turner called out to the boys when he noticed them watching. "What do you think about all this?" he asked. "Makes a bit of a difference, doesn't it?"

"Don't fink the cows like it much," Tommy said watching the one nearest to him kick one back leg hard into the air. "Does it 'urt 'em?"

"No." Mr Turner laughed. "They're getting used to

it. Saves our hands and our time. Jo and Alfredo'll be able to put their feet up an hour earlier.''

They climbed on to the high fence and watched the proceedings, keeping one eye on Alfredo and wondering whether or not he was going to tell them anything.

As he moved into the room with the milk containers he half beckoned them with his head and very slowly and carefully they climbed down from the fence and followed him.

Alfredo wasted no time. ''I hava the plana,'' he said and walked across the room as though he wasn't really speaking to them.

Charlie swallowed hard. ''What is it?'' he asked in a voice that came out much squeakier than he intended.

''I go to Melbourne. I find a shipa.''

''How are you going to get to Melbourne?'' they asked almost together.

''In the airplane. You help.'' He looked at Peter.

''Gee, I can't help you do that. What do you want to go to Melbourne for? Why not Sydney? There are ships there.''

''I know. Go to Africa from Melbourne.''

''Who told you that?'' Peter asked, surprised.

''Old paper in barn. I go Melbourne. In the airplane. I go Africa in shipa, I go Italy.''

They heard Mr Turner talking to Jo outside and thought he was coming into the room, so they pretended to be busily watching the milk pouring into the container.

''You tell me,'' Alfredo went on talking, ''time, day, airplane goes to Melbourne.''

Jo and the farmer came in to see how much milk had come into the container, so the boys slipped out, waved goodbye and raced over the farmyard.

''Come on,'' Peter called, ''we haven't got time to look for eggs, Tommy.''

They picked up their bikes and walked with them to the top of the drive.

"How am I supposed to find out about the planes? Write to General Macarthur? I don't know anything about them."

"Your dad does," Charlie said.

Tommy looked thoughtful. "It'd be better to go by train. Why don't we tell 'im that?"

"I don't think we'll tell him anything," Peter answered.

"We said we would."

"No we didn't. We just sort of said we might. We didn't even know what he wanted the atlas for."

"Charlie and I did."

They got on their bikes and rode slowly down the dirt driveway.

"I'll just kind of see if I can talk to Dad," Peter said after a while, "but he'll want to know what I'm asking for."

"Then you'll have to think of something. Talk as though it's just not very important or something."

"Yeah?" Peter pedalled off in front of the other two. "That's all right for you. I'll probably end up getting put in gaol."

They rode to their homes and put their bikes away. That evening after dinner each of them sat quietly and listened to the wireless. Charlie and Tommy listened to "Yes, What?" because Mrs Calder and Mrs Walters let them choose their programmes. Peter half listened to the BBC news because his father and his grandfather wanted to hear it, but all the way through he wondered just how he was going to approach his father and ask him about the planes. The more he thought about it, the harder it became.

"I wish he'd just go to Italy and leave us out of it," he

said to himself and wished his father would turn off the news and let him turn on to "Yes, What?"

There were too many things cropping up and interrupting his time. Things were getting too complicated.

"Hey, Dad," he said at last, "can I listen to 'Yes, What?'"

His father sighed, turned the switch and Peter leaned back in his chair to listen to the last five minutes of his favourite programme.

11 NOT A GAME

That night, Tommy had a nightmare. "Mam!" he called staring into the blackness. "Essie!" He couldn't move, he was jammed into a ball in that blackness.

His aunt came and held him close. Then she lay down beside him on the bed until he went back to sleep.

The next morning Jack Martin drove his taxi up to the pump to get his ration of petrol.

"Oh it's a worry," Mrs Walters told him, "but what Miss Leslie doesn't understand is that he needs me. I'm the only one he's got except for his father and he's not much use to him at the moment."

"She'll settle down," he reassured her. "She's got a bee in her bonnet now, but she'll get over it."

"No she won't," Mrs Walters said angrily. "She'll talk to that Miss Hume as sure as anything and now that Bill's gone away she'll have more time to think about Tommy."

"One step at a time," he said. "We'll wait and when we need to act, we'll act."

"You're on my side then?" She brightened.

"Of course I'm on your side, Marion, and Tommy's

too. I don't think he should leave Tiboorie, planes or no planes.''

"Good.'' She thrust the petrol hose into the tank of his car and stood waiting while it filled. "I'm ready. Any time she wants to start a battle, I'm ready to fight.''

Jack Martin laughed and reached for his wallet in his hip pocket. "One war's enough, Marion. We can leave the fighting to the men in the forces. By the way, did you hear anything about last night on Sydney Harbour?''

"No.'' The tank filled and she put the hose back on the side of the pump. "Too busy worrying about Tommy.''

"Did you listen to the wireless this morning?''

"Yes. Didn't hear anything.''

"Whatever happened they're keeping it to themselves. Margaret's cousin Jenny rang up and said there was a real commotion down there. Air-raid sirens, guns, searchlights, bombs. Something happened all right.''

"Bombs?''

"Well, shells more likely, but I don't know where they would have come from. Couldn't have been an air-raid, we'd have heard about that. Can't see how the Japs could have got down so far south as Sydney.''

"Wasn't the Coral Sea battle supposed to stop all that? Send them all packing back to Japan?''

"Not quite, Marion. It was a pretty good victory but we're not going to win the war overnight.''

"It all sounds a bit close for my liking,'' she said taking his money and putting in into her apron pocket.

"Couldn't be much closer. Ralph Andrews is going to ring from the Air Force station.''

"Well give me a ring when you find out.'' She turned to go then came back. "Where would the shells have come from?''

"Battleship if they got in close enough. I don't think they've been taking the Japs too seriously down there in

Sydney, even though they have a blackout. They're too new at it.''

He slammed the taxi door behind him and drove slowly off.

In the playground everyone was trying to outdo the other with news about the night's activities in Sydney. Excitement raced through them. Stories of what could have happened grew and grew. Frank Harris knew for a fact that a ship had been sunk and, as most of the children knew that at least one American warship was in the harbour, apart from Australian ones, they tried to guess which one it might have been.

The bell rang and all the talking stopped, but once inside the classroom everyone felt restless. From his desk near the window Peter saw his grandfather drive up in his taxi and blurted out, ''What's Grandad coming here for?''

Miss Leslie stood on the platform near her desk and called sharply. ''That will do, Peter. Sit down at once.''

He sat down and nudged Charlie with his elbow. In a few moments there was a knock on the classroom door. Miss Leslie silenced them with a look and walked across to open it.

She and Mr Martin spoke for a few moments, then she came back into the room and walked up to Peter and Charlie's desk.

''You're wanted at home, Charlie,'' she told him quietly. ''Take your bag. Mr Martin's waiting.''

Charlie looked up in surprise. ''Why?''

''Mr Martin will explain, Charlie. Here, don't forget your pencils.''

''Can I go too?'' Peter asked quickly jumping to his feet.

"No, you can't. Sit down Peter."

Peter sat down, muttering under his breath. "Gosh, he's my friend and it's my grandfather."

Charlie didn't speak until he and Mr Martin were sitting in the taxi. "Is Mum all right?"

"Well—she's a bit worried, Charlie. It seems that some Japanese submarines got into Sydney Harbour last night and sent a few torpedoes off in all directions."

"Submarines! What's that got to do with Mum?"

"One of them fired a torpedo and it hit the ferry Tim was on, the *Kuttabul*."

"Hit it?" Charlie wondered what that meant. He'd seen warships hit by torpedoes at the pictures and they'd usually blown up and sunk. Sailors in the water. Lifeboats. Men wounded, killed, drowning. But Tim was real. Would it be the same if it were true? If it happened to someone you knew?

"What happened to Tim?" His throat felt tight and sore.

"That's what we don't know, Charlie. Not yet."

Mr Martin turned into the street leading to the Calder home. "They're saying what the torpedoes missed, but not much about what they hit."

"How do you know they hit the ferry, then?"

"Got a mate on Garden Island. He said it sank. He's trying to find out about Tim."

They went into the house and found Peter's mother sitting with Mrs Calder, a cold cup of tea on the table beside her. Charlie rushed over and flung his arms around his mother's neck.

"Tim's a real good swimmer, Mum," he said, searching for comfort for her and for himself. "He could swim anywhere."

He sat on the floor beside her and Jack Martin lowered himself on to the sofa next to Mrs Andrews.

"What are we going to do?" Charlie asked, wondering why they were just sitting there.

"Your mother wants to go down to Sydney but I think she ought to wait a bit." He turned to Mrs Calder. "Don Black'll ring as soon as he finds out anything, Helen. You'll have all the time in the train worrying, and you might not have anything to worry about at all."

"I want to be down there, Jack. I can't just sit here and wait."

They argued for a while and then agreed that Mrs Calder would catch the two o'clock train and Charlie would stay with the Andrews until she got back.

Mrs Andrews made some sandwiches for lunch and they all sat, waiting for the sound of the telephone bell.

Just after one o'clock it rang. Mr Martin answered it and shouted down the receiver to his friend in Sydney. "Yes," he said. "No. What do you know about that! That'll scare the pants off those Navy blokes. Yes, Helen's coming down on the two o'clock. She'll be able to see him all right? Okay, Don. Thank you very much. We appreciate it."

He turned back to the three anxious faces waiting to hear what he said.

"The ferry sank, but Tim got off in time. A torpedo all right. Now, wait a minute, Helen. He's hurt, but not badly. His arm, Don said. He saw him up at the hospital."

"He's in hospital?" Charlie's mother sank down again on her chair.

"Of course, he's in hospital, Helen. They'd have taken him up to the hospital even if he hadn't been hurt. Routine."

They all breathed a sigh of relief. Mrs Calder hurried into her bedroom to pack a suitcase, Mrs Andrews began washing-up and Charlie sat next to Mr Martin.

"What happened to the submarines, Mr Martin?" Charlie asked. "How many were there? Did they sink any other ships?"

Mr Martin put his hand on Charlie's shoulder. "Wait a minute now. One question at a time. They don't know how many there were, three or four, but they know at least one was sunk. Used depth charges. No other ships were damaged. It seems they aimed for the American cruisers, but the torpedoes went under them, then under the *Kuttabul* and hit the wall next to it. That was enough to sink it straight off."

"How did they get into the harbour? I thought there was a big net or something across the channel so nothing could get past."

"There is. Called a boom. That's the mystery. We don't know how they got in, but we understand enough about the Japs to know that they didn't worry about how they'd get out. Their job was to get the American cruisers."

"And they missed. Gee, I bet Tim got a fright."

His mother drove off with Mr Martin in the taxi and Mrs Andrews took Charlie back home with her. Inside she went to the telephone and talked to Pam, and Charlie played with Peter's model planes until Peter arrived home.

Peter had already heard about Tim. The news had raced through the township and Miss Leslie stopped her lesson to tell them everything she had learnt from the wireless in the headmaster's office, the newspaper and various phone calls. But she hadn't known anything about the extent of Tim's injuries.

The evening paper told them that each of the submarines had been manned by two Japanese. Midget submarines. They had entered the harbour, according to the Navy, behind a ferry coming through the boom, and at least one had been sunk by depth charges.

But no one seemed to know very much about the men on board the *Kuttabul*.

After dinner that night the whole Andrews family crowded around the wireless, listening to all the news programmes, but felt they knew more about what had happened than they were being told by the announcers.

Pam wanted to go down to Sydney to be with Tim, but her father put his foot down. She had to wait until they heard from Mrs Calder.

The phone rang at about eight o'clock that night. Mrs Calder told them that she had seen Tim and he appeared to be all right except for an injury to his elbow. He had to stay in hospital for a few days and then he'd probably come home on sick leave. She wasn't sure, but had thought she would come back the following day. She didn't think it necessary for Pam to come, as Tim would be home soon. When her father told her, Pam rushed off into her room crying.

Mrs Andrews stood up and followed her, and Peter rolled his eyes at Charlie, knowing that the crisis in his sister's bedroom was going to be hard to manage.

It might be a good time to talk about the planes going to Melbourne, he thought. His father wouldn't be concentrating too hard, half listening to what Mrs Andrews was saying to Pam.

"Dad?"

"What is it, Peter?"

"Are there more planes coming in and out of the station now than there used to be?"

"I suppose you can say that," he answered. "What do you want to know for?"

"Oh nothing. Just wondered."

"Where do they go mostly, Mr Andrews?" Charlie asked innocently.

"Where do they go?" Mr Andrews looked puzzled.

"All over the place. Sydney, Brisbane, Melbourne, Tocumwal, Amberley. Some go further north."

"Do they go to New Guinea?" Peter asked.

"Yes. They have to refuel a couple of times if they do."

Charlie began to gain confidence. "Can they go all the way to Melbourne without refuelling anywhere?"

"Yes."

Peter's grandfather joined in the conversation, putting down his newspaper.

"You thinking about Tommy? It's the southbound planes that fly over the town. That's right, isn't it Ralph?"

"Yes. Any other direction and they stay on the eastern side."

"Yes," Peter put in quickly and pushed his foot against Charlie's leg. "We're thinking about Tommy. He has one of his fits when they go over the school."

"Peter," his grandfather said sharply, "fits isn't the right word. He gets upset when he hears them."

"How often do they go to Melbourne, then?" Peter asked.

"Good Heavens above, Peter, I don't know." His father picked up the newspaper. "A couple of times a week. You hear them."

"Yes, but I didn't know they went to Melbourne. Do they go at special times?"

"What are you getting at, Peter?" His father was beginning to sound exasperated.

Charlie's eyes brightened as he thought of something. "If we knew when they were going to Melbourne we could tell Tommy and then he'd know and he probably wouldn't take a...get upset so much."

"It's not a bad idea," Mr Martin nodded, agreeing. "All right, I'll look into it. They don't go on a regular time-table, they're not buses." He rattled the paper.

"They've got a job to do and little boys like Tommy, unfortunately, don't come into it."

"Will you try, Dad?"

"I'll think about it." He went on reading the paper and Mrs Andrews came out of Pam's room and signalled to the boys that it was time to go to bed.

In the twin beds in Peter's room they whispered to one another.

"We didn't get very far, but it was better than nothing."

Charlie pulled the blankets up under his chin. "I was pretty clever saying that about Tommy, wasn't I?"

"Yeah." Peter thought he should give him credit because it might be a good way of finding out a bit more. If he thought it would help Tommy maybe his father would tell them just what days and times the planes went south to Melbourne. They'd have to wait, but at least they'd made a start.

Peter settled down on to his pillow. "We'd better go to sleep. If we get up early we can talk about it outside. Don't forget—walls have ears."

And they both turned over and were asleep in a few minutes.

Tim came home on sick leave and Charlie went back to school, but nothing Peter or Tommy could say helped him feel any better. Things at home were very bad. The news had come through that nineteen men, a lot of them Tim's friends, had been killed on the ferry and eight injured. His arm was in plaster and he wouldn't talk about what had happened and wouldn't go out anywhere in case people talked to him. Charlie was finding it very difficult watching his mother trying to help Tim and getting no result.

"He's been as cranky as anything," Charlie told them. "He won't talk—well, not much anyway."

"Does his arm hurt?" Peter asked.

"I dunno. He doesn't talk about it, but Mum's got to do things for him and he doesn't like it."

The three boys sat and imagined what it would be like to have their right arms in plaster and decided to themselves that it would certainly stop them from doing a lot of things. Eating wouldn't be easy.

"Pam's worse than Tim, I bet," Peter told them. "She won't talk to anyone."

"Come round to my place," Tommy said, "Auntie Marion goes on like a babbling brook."

They did decide to go to Tommy's after school and were there when Mr Martin called in. He had seen their bikes as he passed by after taking some Air Force officers to the railway station.

They all sat outside on the steps leading into the shop.

"Things not going too well at home, Charlie?" he asked, taking out his pipe and pushing the tobacco down with his thumb.

"I thought it'd be good with Tim at home for a bit, but it's awful," Charlie told him.

"'Is arm's goin' to get all right, isn't it, Mr Martin?" Tommy asked as Mr Martin lit his pipe and drew in deep breaths.

They waited for an answer.

Mr Martin looked at the glowing tobacco in his pipe, gave a small suck to keep it going and then took it out of his mouth to speak.

"It might not be much good to him, that's the trouble. Elbows are funny things. Hard to mend."

They all looked up questioning him, and trying to fathom the full meaning of what he said. If you were fighting the enemy and you couldn't use your right arm, you certainly wouldn't be much use—that was easy to understand. But what would you do instead?

When Tommy asked, Mr Martin chose his words carefully. "I guess they wouldn't want you at all. Not much use to anyone if you can't pull a trigger."

"But the Navy's different," Peter said.

"Not that different," his grandfather replied. "The guns might be a bit bigger, but you still need to pull the trigger."

Charlie suddenly understood the long silences at home and Tim's despair. "Mightn't they want Tim any more?" he asked.

"Not if his arm doesn't work, Charlie."

"He'd have to stay home." The seriousness of it all came to Charlie as he spoke. "He couldn't go into the Army either, or the Air Force. He'd have to go back to the bank. Gosh."

"And it wasn't even a real war," Peter put in.

"It was pretty real down there on the harbour, Peter," his grandfather told him. "Nineteen young men were killed, apart from the Japanese. Tim was a hero just the same as all the other men who go off to war are heroes. I just hope it's all over by the time you three grow up. Tommy knows something about it, I do, now Tim does. You and Charlie might be lucky enough to miss it all."

Mr Martin puffed on his pipe, his thoughts drifting.

"I don't want to miss it," Peter said. "You tell all those terrific stories about France in the last war, Grandad. The Somme and Pos—"

"Pozières."

"Pozières and those places."

"I only tell you the bits I don't mind remembering, Peter. A lot of things happened that I don't talk about, or think about if I can help it." He put his pipe back in his mouth and puffed. "War's not a game," he said.

"You wanted to go, Grandad," Peter insisted.

"That was 1914. Wouldn't have in 1940. I'd have known what it was all about."

"What if the Japs land in Sydney and then come up here?" Charlie sat tense, waiting for the reply.

"Then it would be our war, wouldn't it?" He gazed into space and then back to the three boys sitting beside him. "It's best not to think about that. Best not. It's better if we put our faith in men like Bill. He and his mates have got those Japs marked now." He stood up. "And don't forget your Auntie Marion, Tommy." He smiled and walked over to his taxi. "She'd give them something to think about, that's for sure."

12   RIVER RESCUE

"Hey!" Peter called from across the street. "I've got it."

He'd been searching for Tommy and Charlie all the morning.

"Got what?"

Peter ran across the street to join them. But Charlie hurried on. He had to pick up a parcel for his mother from the draper before the shops closed at 12 o'clock. "Come on," he said, and beckoned Peter to follow.

They walked past the butcher shop, the grocer shop and outside the post office Peter stopped them.

"What you on about?" Tommy asked.

"*S-sh*," Peter warned and he led them to the far end of the post office steps.

"Dad told me about the planes. The ones going to Melbourne."

Charlie gasped in surprise. "Didn't think he would."

"Well, he only told me about two regular ones. Said the others came and went all over the place."

"Two's enough. We've got to tell Alfredo."

Tommy started down the steps. "Let's go now."

"No." Charlie walked on. "I've got to get the parcel. The shops'll close. He can wait a bit."

"Meet you up the farm after lunch then," Peter said, going along with them down the footpath.

"Don't you tell 'im 'fore we get there," Tommy warned. "We've all got to know."

"I won't," Peter said holding his secret and wishing he could race up to the farm without them.

Charlie turned into the entrance of the draper's shop. "What do you think he'll do?" he whispered.

"Go to Italy of course," Tommy answered and as they reached the menswear counter and stood waiting Peter uttered a loud, "*S-sh.*"

The shopkeeper bent down behind the counter then handed Charlie a brown-paper parcel.

"Here we are, Charlie," he said. "This one's the size your mother wanted."

Charlie took the parcel and walked out with it under his arm. The others followed.

"It's a jumper for Tim," he explained as they reached the street. "He won't wear his Navy one and his old ones are too small."

They started walking towards home.

"Isn't he going back?" Peter asked.

"They won't tell him till his sick leave is up. Another week. Come on, we've got to hurry."

Alfredo listened to Peter and wrote down the times the regular planes left for Melbourne.

"Now I make the plana," he said decisively, folded the paper and put it into his pocket.

They'd all met at the barn soon after lunch and now the boys waited near the barn door for Alfredo to tell them what he intended to do, but, without another word, he picked up his jacket and walked out the door.

They followed him up the path to the dairy for some of

the way. Then realising he wasn't going to stop, let alone
talk, they slowed down and eventually stopped. They
looked at each other helplessly.

"Do you think he's going to tell us about his plan?"
Charlie asked, disappointed.

"He 'asn't made it yet," Tommy reminded him.

"He'll probably go and join the Japs and come back
here and bomb us or something," Peter said, suddenly
feeling guilty about the whole exercise.

Tommy put his hands in his pockets and started off
along the path again. "'E only wants to get back to 'is
family."

"That's what he tells us," Peter said. "I wish I hadn't
told him now."

They walked past the barn, climbed the fence, walked
through the paddock and reached the river.

Now it was winter, the whole area looked different.
The water ran much quicker as there had been heavy rain
during the week, the grass on the banks grew high and
raggedy and the grey skies made the green of the trees
look dark and uninviting.

They picked up stones and skimmed them over the
water, but they weren't really interested.

"Wish we could go for a swim," Charlie said without
much enthusiasm.

"You'd get froze," Tommy said, shivering.

Charlie looked about him, stood up and walked along
the side of the bank. He'd remembered about Tim's
canoe and knew it must be somewhere because it wasn't
at home. Tim sometimes left it there and he must have
forgotten about it. He found it at last and pushed it down
the bank towards the others.

"Let's play submarines," he called.

"Okay." Peter jumped up. "You be a submarine and
I'll be a Jap Zero."

He ran over to the nearest tree and started to climb it. "You can be the *Kuttabul*, Tommy."

He found a spot in the high branches of the tree which hung over the river, pulled off sticks and leaves and dropped them down on to the canoe.

Charlie paddled out of the way and Tommy sat on the bank watching, but not interested. He wondered about Alfredo and what his next move would be.

Peter grew tired of throwing sticks and looked around for something else, saw some logs on the bank and climbed down from the tree.

"I'm going to be a destroyer," he called, and pushed one of the logs out into the water. "I've got you in my sights and I'm sending off a torpedo." The log headed towards the canoe and Peter turned back to find another.

"Look out!" Tommy shouted, alarmed. "You'll sink 'im."

"He's a Jap," Peter called back, turning around to see the result of his work.

Charlie twisted the canoe from one direction to another. "I'm doing evasive tactics," he called.

Tommy saw the tip of the submerged log first and he shouted at the top of his voice, but it was too late. The canoe hit it, overturned and Charlie spilled out into the water.

Peter and Tommy stood on the bank, immobile, waiting for Charlie to come to the surface.

The canoe moved down the rapidly flowing water, upside down, but there was no sign of Charlie.

"Charlie," Peter yelled. He pulled off his jumper and shoes and threw himself into the water. He swam out to where the canoe had overturned then he dived down into the muddy brown water. He came up spluttering.

"Tommy, come and help!" he shouted.

Tommy saw the wide expanse of water in front of him,

Peter's wet hair flattened on his frightened face. What could he do?

"Tommy!" Peter called again.

Tommy picked up a long branch, balanced himself along a fallen tree trunk protruding into the river and pushed it out towards Peter. Peter held it for a moment, then they both saw Charlie appear on the surface, the force of the water pushing him down the river past them.

Peter let go the branch and swam towards him. He grabbed him by the shoulders, but the water swirled around them and he almost lost his grip.

"Hurry, Tommy," Peter yelled.

Tommy rushed back on to the bank. He'd have to go up to the farm for help. His voice choked as he called back to Peter.

"I can't swim," he almost sobbed. "I'll 'ave to get someone."

He ran like lightning towards the farm, shouting at the top of his voice. "Mr Turner! Alfredo! Jo!"

Alfredo heard him, ran out into the open and called, "Tommy! What's the trouble?"

Tommy pointed down to the river. Alfredo grabbed a piece of rope and raced towards him. Jo followed and in the distance Mr Turner climbed the dairy fence and ran as fast as he could go across the paddock.

"It's Charlie and Peter," Tommy stammered out to Alfredo as best he could. "In the river."

He couldn't see them anywhere when they arrived at the river. Tommy pulled Alfredo after him and they pushed their way through the growth on the banks, searching the muddy water, the banks on each side, all around the broken branches half submerged in the waters.

Suddenly he saw something. "There!" Tommy yelled. "There, Alfredo."

Alfredo pulled off his boots and plunged into the water. Peter had one hand on a drifting branch, the other around Charlie. Alfredo reached them, left Peter holding on to the tree and swam with Charlie to the bank. Tommy reached down and together they pulled him on to the flat grass. Alfredo slipped back into the water and swam out to Peter.

Peter scrambled up the bank followed by Alfredo and they both collapsed on to the grass as Jo and Mr Turner raced up to them.

"Go for your life back to the farm," Mr Turner said to Tommy. "Tell Mrs Turner to ring Doc Jenkins. Tell him he can get his car along this far. Bring back a couple of blankets."

Tommy had a quick look at Charlie, lying still and quiet. His eyes were closed and a large purple lump on the side of his head was oozing bright red blood. He ran off as fast as he could towards the farm.

He and Mrs Turner arrived back at the river with the blankets just before the doctor arrived in his car and when Tommy saw Charlie's eyes open and Peter sitting beside him he breathed a great sigh of relief.

Dr Jenkins quickly opened his bag and began examining the two boys. In a few minutes, Jack Martin's taxi came rumbling along the bank and stopped. Jack jumped out and ran across to them.

"What in the name of heaven's been happening?" he cried, looking at the two dripping wet boys.

"Charlie fell out of the canoe," Tommy told him. "Peter went in after him."

Peter looked up. "You weren't much help."

Tommy bit his bottom lip.

"Not much he could do, if he couldn't swim," Mr Martin said as he knelt down beside Charlie. "How are they, Paul?" he asked the doctor.

"Charlie's got a bit knocked about. Better get them both home." The doctor and Alfredo helped Charlie to his feet.

"Wait a minute." Mr Martin thought for a moment. "Charlie's mum's got enough on her plate. She'd better not see him like this. What if we go up to the house? Might be better."

They carried Charlie to the back of the doctor's car and Peter climbed in beside him. Tommy started to join them, but Peter put out his arm and stopped him.

"He's my friend, not yours."

Tommy walked away and sat in the back of the taxi between Alfredo and Jo.

At the house Mrs Turner put Charlie to bed and wrapped Peter in Bill's dressing gown. Mr Turner made tea and everyone sat around the kitchen fire. Soon the warmth of the room began to dry out the dampness and Alfredo put down his mug and explained in his broken English that he would go down to his quarters and change.

"We're proud of you, Alfredo." Mr Turner stood up and opened the door for him. "Another few minutes and they might have drowned. The river gives you a bit of a shock sometimes. It can flow fast."

Alfredo nodded and smiled.

"Alfredo lives near the water back in Salerno," Mr Turner went on. "Big family he's got there. Wine growers. That right Alfredo?"

Alfredo smiled and nodded again.

"Let him get out of those wet clothes, Bob," Mr Martin cut in. "The man'll die of cold with all your talking."

The farmer put his hand on Alfredo's shoulder. "We've got a lot to thank you for Alfredo, you did a good job."

Jo stood up and the two men walked out the kitchen door.

"You need to have a healthy respect for water," Bob Turner said as he sat down to finish his tea.

Tommy agreed, but said nothing. He had never wanted to swim and hadn't worried about it until he came to Tiboorie. He had lived in a land surrounded by sea, but that was for ships and boats, not people. Now he wished with all his heart that he'd gone to the swimming baths like some of his friends. Then he wouldn't have let Charlie down. He could have saved him, instead of Peter.

Peter sat huddled in the dressing gown feeling the warmth of the fire. His grandfather stood up to go and told them that he'd take Tommy home, get some clothes for Peter and Charlie and come back later.

Tommy sat next to him in the front of the taxi cold and unhappy and wondering what Mr Martin would say to him.

"Quick thinking getting Alfredo, Tommy," he said at last.

"I should've gone in too," he murmured, his head down on his chest.

Mr Martin moved about in his seat and changed his grip on the steering wheel. He'd been able to piece together what had happened gradually and knew that Tommy didn't like the kind of game the two boys had been playing and wondered just how involved he'd been. If he couldn't swim then there was no way he should have gone into the water.

"I got a stick, but that wasn't much good."

"You did the right thing, Tommy. You got help."

"They might've drowned while I went."

"But they didn't, did they?"

"No. Nearly though. Peter'll think I'm scared. He always thinks I'm scared."

Mr Martin peered out along the road as he drove. "Well, you don't want to worry too much about what Peter thinks."

"I do though, Mr Martin." Tears spurted out of his eyes and he turned his head into the rough sleeve of Mr Martin's coat. Jack Martin turned the taxi into the Walters' garage and pulled it to a stop. He put his arm around the boy and Tommy sobbed.

Mrs Walters came rushing out of the house. She'd been waiting for them ever since Mrs Turner had spoken to her on the phone. "You're not hurt are you, Tommy?" she asked anxiously as she flung the car door out. "Oh, Tommy...oh, Tommy."

She helped him out of the car. "Oh, Tommy, you're all wet and cold. Are you coming in Jack?" she said all in one breath.

"No, Marion, got to get dry clothes back to the boys. Look after him."

"You're not hurt, are you, Tommy?" she asked again as Mr Martin drove off towards Charlie's home.

He wasn't hurt, he wasn't even wet. He walked inside wishing that he'd come home bedraggled and soaking and with everyone saying how brave he'd been rescuing Charlie and nearly drowning himself. But he had just added to the mounting list of things against him, and sooner or later he'd have to face up to Peter. He knew he wasn't a coward, but that would be what Peter thought. He just hoped that Charlie wouldn't feel the same way.

Charlie had to stay home from school and on the first day without him Tommy rode to school by himself. Peter didn't speak to him all day.

When the bell rang in the afternoon Miss Leslie asked

him to stay behind and he waited by her desk while the others filed out of the classroom.

She asked him about Charlie and how the accident happened on the river. He didn't say how the canoe turned over or that Peter had been pushing logs out into the water, but he told her that Alfredo had been the one who rescued the two of them. He didn't know whether she knew he couldn't swim because she moved the conversation around to what she really wanted to say. It was about the welfare officer, Miss Hume.

"I've asked her to come up and visit, Tommy," she said, "just to see how you're getting on."

"I'm all right," he mumbled.

"We need somebody who really understands to tell us that Tommy," she said, "and Miss Hume is trained to do that."

Her words seemed to be floating away as though she wasn't really talking to him at all. He'd failed everything he'd tried to do and now someone was going to interfere in his life again. Miss Hume represented authority and authority was a huge brick wall that people like him could never climb over.

When she'd finished Tommy rushed out to his bike, rode to the corner, got on to the dirt road and with head down he pedalled towards the farm.

There was only one thing he could do. He would go to Africa and find his dad. And he'd go as far as he could with Alfredo.

13 TOMMY AND CHARLIE

He arrived at the farm breathless, dropped his bike with a rattle by the dairy fence and raced into the building. Alfredo wasn't there, but he found Mrs Turner looking very worried. She called out to him.

"Hello there, Tommy. Have you seen Alfredo?"

"No," he answered, but didn't add that he had come specially to see him.

She had been looking around the farm all afternoon. Mr Turner had gone down to the paddocks, which meant Jo had had to bring the cows up for milking by himself.

No one could understand it. He'd been waiting to get a letter from Italy for months and two had arrived for him that morning. He'd gone off to the barn to read them and no one had seen him since.

"It's all a mystery," Mrs Turner told him shaking her head as she walked away towards the house.

Tommy ran through the dairy to the other side. Alfredo must have gone without saying anything. The thought shocked him. He'd gone without even saying goodbye.

He found Jo, but he didn't have anything to tell him.
He just shrugged his shoulders when Tommy asked and
spread out his hands. He knew nothing.

So Tommy got on his bike and rode away from the
farm, back to the main road, and down the street to
Charlie's house.

Once there he ran up the path, straight through the
open front door and in Charlie's bedroom. He closed the
door behind him. Charlie was sitting up in bed building
a meccano bridge. The lump on his head had changed to
a deep purple and his half-closed eye was puffed up with
browny-yellow skin.

Tommy sat down, and suddenly he didn't know what
to say. He hadn't seen Charlie since the accident and he
didn't know how Charlie felt about him.

Charlie sensed it. "I didn't know you couldn't swim,"
he said.

Tommy didn't answer.

"If you had we might've all got drowned."

Tommy looked at him sideways. "What do you
mean?"

"You would've gone in too and there wouldn't have
been anyone there to get Alfredo."

"I could've saved you."

"I'm glad you got Alfredo, Tommy."

Charlie busily put a nut on to the piece of meccano he
held. "It was the best thing to do," he added.

Tommy felt a great weight lift off his shoulders. He
picked up two pieces of meccano and a nut.

"Anything happened while I've been in bed?" Charlie
asked.

"That's what I came to tell you about," Tommy said
dramatically, "Alfredo's gone."

Charlie learned forward. "Gone where?" he gasped.
"Italy?"

Tommy motioned him to speak quietly. "He must've," he whispered. "He's disappeared."

"Disappeared?" Charlie suddenly relaxed and said in a relieved voice. "Well, if he's gone, he's gone. It hasn't got anything to do with us any more."

Tommy moved further up the bed towards Charlie. "But I wanted to go with him."

"You what!" The effect on Charlie was devastating. "What do you want to go to Italy for?"

"Not Italy. I'm going to Africa," he said, "to me dad."

"You can't do that."

"Yes I can. I can't stay 'ere any longer. And I know all about ships and I know 'ow you can stowaway in 'em, 'cause we used to talk about it when I was coming out and we'd look for places to hide, and I knew where you could get food and everyfink."

Charlie lay back on the pillows trying to work it all out. At last he spoke, quietly. "What about your auntie?"

"She won't have to worry about me any more. Not when I've gone."

Charlie felt dizzy. He had never thought it possible that Tommy would go away from Tiboorie by himself. He could imagine Alfredo stowing away on a plane and then on a ship, but not Tommy.

The pieces of meccano fell off the bed on to the floor with a loud rattle which brought Mrs Calder to the bedroom.

She fussed around Charlie, tucking in the blankets and straightening his pillows, then she turned to Tommy and with her arm on his shoulder she walked with him to the door. Charlie had to rest, she explained. As he left Tommy called to Charlie that he'd come in to see him on his way to school in the morning.

"Don't do anything before then," Charlie pleaded,

"and don't forget to come in. I'll be waiting from seven o'clock."

Tommy had a lot of planning to do. It all ran around in his head as he ate his dinner. But his aunt kept telling him about what she'd heard about the Italian prisoner-of-war escaping and he couldn't concentrate. He helped her wash-up and then sat on the lounge with a book pretending to read. Without Alfredo he would have to think everything out differently. He'd be on his own, but he knew he could do it. It would just take time to get it all together. He'd make a list and put down everything he'd need. And he'd find out about the trains. It would just need working out. He just wished he'd been able to talk to Alfredo.

Tommy told his aunt he'd be calling in to see Charlie on his way to school and left home at about half past seven.

He settled himself in Charlie's bedroom and began talking about all the things he had planned during the night.

Just as they were beginning to talk in earnest, they heard voices outside and Peter marched into the room. He dropped his school case on the floor with a crash.

"Peter," Mrs Calder called, "not so much noise."

Peter winced and said quietly, "Did you hear about Alfredo?"

"Yes," Charlie said and decided to get out of bed and put on his dressing gown. "He went to Italy."

"No he didn't," Peter said.

Tommy and Charlie stood—Charlie with his dressing gown in his hand—gazing wide-eyed at Peter and waiting for him to go on.

"Uncle Bob rang Grandad from the farm last night.

They couldn't find him because he'd gone for a great long walk—along the river.''

"For the whole day?" Charlie exclaimed.

Tommy didn't speak. He just listened as Peter went on.

"He got this letter from Italy and you know his wife and that signing papers he told us about?"

Both boys nodded.

"Well in the letter someone told him that she hadn't ever signed the papers. So he's not married!" Peter relaxed on the bed after delivering this final thrust.

"Gee," Charlie felt concerned, "is she going to marry him when he gets back?"

"No. She married someone else—properly, in a church."

"Then he 'asn't gone yet?" Tommy said. Now he could go with Alfredo after all. He began to feel excited. It'd be easier for them both if they went together. Tommy could buy the tickets and do the talking for Alfredo and read the signs and notices. Alfredo would need him. He had to tell him.

His excitement bubbled over and for a moment he forget about Peter. He handed Charlie his dressing gown and helped him put it on.

"Cor lumme," he said, "now we can go togever after all."

Peter looked from one to the other, frowning. "Go where?"

Tommy faced him defiantly. "Africa."

"Like wax," Peter flung back. "How could you go to Africa when you can't even listen to the sound of an aeroplane engine without throwing a fit."

"I'm not going to get an aeroplane. I'm going to get a train. It's better."

"Huh. See, you're too scared to go in a plane."

Tommy rubbed his hands on the front of his pants, itching to reach out and punch Peter. He glanced towards the door, knowing Mrs Calder would come in as soon as she heard any noise. He sat back on the bed, and Charlie tied the belt of his dressing gown into a knot and pulled the ends hard.

"You shouldn't say that, Peter," Charlie told him.

"Why not? He is."

"I've been trying to find a way for ages to stop him being scared. If we could do that he could stay here."

Peter didn't answer. He knew he had to tread carefully. Charlie looked awful with his black puffy eye and the rest of his face as white as a sheet. He'd see Tommy at school and find out what he was up to.

But Charlie had started to think about his ideas. "Why don't you do what I said a long time ago, Tommy," Charlie said suddenly. "If you went up close to an aeroplane and touched it and saw it was just an old plane you might not be scared any more and you wouldn't have to go anywhere. Your grandad said that too, Peter."

"He didn't."

"Well, you said that he said you had to face the things you were scared of and that's what Tommy'd be doing."

"He'd faint with fright. Anyway that's not the only thing he's scared of. He's scared of cows and water and everything else around here. I bet he couldn't go within ten feet of a DC3."

"Bet I could." Tommy clenched his fists but kept them by his side. He wasn't scared of Peter and if he didn't stop talking like that, he'd show him.

"Prove it," Peter sneered.

"Go on Tommy," Charlie urged his friend, "we'll all go out there to the Air Force station and sneak into one of the hangars and see if you can do it."

Peter nodded. "Then he can go to Africa and we won't see him any more."

Charlie picked up a piece of meccano and threw it at Peter's head. "You're a creep, Peter. If he can stop getting the shakes he won't have to go to Africa. He can stay here. I don't want you to go, Tommy. I want you to get better and stay."

Peter's head hurt and he rubbed it. He'd show Charlie once and for all what Tommy was really like. He'd take him to the Air Force station, show him the planes and that would be the end of it. Tommy was a scared rat and he'd prove it.

"Come on then," Tommy said, standing up.

"I can't go now," Charlie whispered. "Wait till after school and I'll talk to Mum about going out somewhere."

"I've got to see Alfredo after school," Tommy told him.

"See him when we get back. I'll meet you after school at the corner."

They walked out to the veranda together and Charlie watched Peter and Tommy go to opposite sides of the gate, pick up their bikes and ride off separately. He sighed. If this didn't work he'd just about run out of ideas for getting Tommy better and if it did maybe the three of them could get back to being friends. He certainly hoped so.

14   OUT OF BOUNDS

After school Tommy waited at the corner for Peter who had told him he would pick up Charlie on the way. But Peter rode up alone. He'd called in for Charlie only to find Mrs Calder emphatic that Charlie couldn't leave the house for any reason whatsoever until the end of the week. He knew how Charlie would feel about missing out, so he didn't go in to see him but asked Mrs Calder to tell him he'd call back in an hour.

She didn't ask any questions and he left the house as quickly as he could.

Tommy followed him along the road to the Air Force station, a road he had never ridden along before. There were no planes in the air.

At the gates Peter stopped to talk to one of the guards. Tommy looked across the great flat expanse of ground to the aeroplanes surrounded by sandbags and the big hangars behind them.

Peter signalled him to follow and they rode along the main road through the station. At the spot where the road branched off towards the married men's quarters, they stopped again and Peter quickly turned his bike in the direction of the hangars. At a big patch of trees and gardens Peter got off his bike and rested it against a tree.

"Put your bike next to mine," he said, snapping out the order.

They waited until two men walked into the door of the administration building, then went quickly towards the hangars. Notices blazed in front of Tommy's eyes. NO ENTRY. STRICTLY AUTHORISED PERSONNEL ONLY.

They raced to the doorway and slipped inside. When their eyes became used to the gloom, they saw, about twenty yards from them, the deep grey outline of a DC3 aircraft. Its high tail and wings stretched out into the space of the huge hangar.

"It must've just been serviced," Peter whispered.

Tommy's heart beat so fast he could feel it right through him. His legs shook, but he wasn't going to let Peter know that. "'Ow do you know?" he said as calmly as he could.

"It'd be outside if it hadn't. Come on."

It was quiet and still in the dimly lit hangar.

Peter walked over to the plane, stood up against it and looked around for Tommy. "Come on," he said, "you wanted to come, didn't you?"

Tommy moved a few steps forward. He'd had no idea that a plane could be so big. Once in London he'd seen a crashed German bomber at the end of his street, but it had been a tangled heap of grey metal. He remembered running up to it and just seeing the black cross on the fuselage before a warden pushed him back.

He could see the propeller on one of the two big engines at the front of the wings, the open door at the side of the plane and the tail that seemed to stretch up forever. He walked slowly across the space between where he stood and the plane and stopped beside Peter. He reached out his hand and lightly touched the side, walked under the wing to the front, and back down the side to the steps leading inside. Peter waited, watching him carefully.

"Okay," he said, "I believe you. You're not scared."

"I'm going inside," Tommy said, and started up the steps.

"Hey, wait on," Peter called after him. "You don't have to go that far. Someone'll come in a sec."

"I've got to see what it's like inside."

"Why? Come on, let's get going."

"I've got to know."

Tommy climbed the steps, slowly and carefully. At the door he peered inside and disappeared from Peter's view.

With a bound Peter leapt up the steps and stood inside with him.

"I have to tell Alfredo. I'll go in a plane if he really wants to. Look back there, there's bags and stuff we can hide in."

"There mightn't be any in another plane," Peter reminded him.

"It's mail," Tommy said, "sure to be some in every plane."

He walked down to the pile of dark blue mailbags, looked at the sides of the plane with the webbing seats hanging from the sides of the fuselage and noted the dimness of the area.

"We could hide 'ere easy," he said.

He kicked at the bags and suddenly the darkness disappeared and bright light flooded the hangar. Loud voices called from one side to the other and Peter and Tommy, with one rush, fell on to the mail bags and wormed their way into them.

Three Air Force officers climbed up the steps, strode through the plane to the controls in the front and before they had time to think what was happening someone pushed the steps up into the plane and slammed the door shut. Tommy and Peter peered out from their hiding place among the bags to the dark interior of the plane.

Then they felt it move. The light grew brighter until they could see the sun shining through the round side windows.

"They're pulling us outside," Peter whispered in alarm.

They could hear the crew talking, but couldn't see them for the partition that separated the cabin from the rest of the plane. But the door was open and they could hear the voices. They looked at one another, wondering what they should do. Peter opened his mouth to call out, but just then the sound of the voices from the cabin became stern and crisp.

"They're getting radio permission to take off!" Peter whispered, frightened.

But Tommy didn't hear him. He had disappeared into the soft sacks of mail, his hands over his ears and his body curled into a tight ball.

The plane moved down the tarmac and stopped. The first engine revved up, the second engine revved and the plane raced down the runway. In a few moments they were airborne.

Charlie sat on the front veranda waiting for Peter and Tommy to come back. The doctor said he could go back to school on Monday, but his mother wouldn't let him get dressed and kept telling him that he had to rest. He felt all right and now he was disappointed and annoyed that Peter and Tommy had gone without him. He wondered what would happen when Tommy saw a real plane and whether he had been game enough to touch it.

He wished they'd hurry.

The afternoon wore on and Charlie waited until his

mother came outside looking worried. Mrs Andrews had rung and asked her if she had seen Peter and now Mrs Walters was on the phone about Tommy.

He couldn't tell her that he knew where they were, or thought he knew. That would mean real trouble. So he said he didn't know. He really didn't know. Not at that very moment. They might be at the airfield, or on their way home, or Tommy might even had had a fit. No, he didn't know where they were.

Mrs Calder rang Mrs Walters and Mrs Walters rang the farm. No one had seen them there. She rang the railway station in case they had ridden past.

Mrs Andrews rang her husband at the Air Force station and Mr Martin got into his taxi and cruised slowly around the streets, then drove down the road that led to the river.

The engines of the plane droned on steadily and the crew talked together over the noise. Peter pushed off the bags on top of him, stretched up and pulled a bag away from Tommy. Tommy reached out and pulled it back.

''Tommy?'' Peter put his hand on Tommy's shoulder and shook him gently. ''Tommy,'' he pleaded. ''Please be all right.''

Tommy took one hand away from his ear.

Peter whispered desperately. ''Are you all right?'' Tell me.''

Slowly Tommy sat up. He took the other hand away from his ear and looked around him. He saw the bright blue sky through the window and he squeezed his eyes shut as he listened to the drone of the engines.

''They don't sound the same,'' he said at last, ''not when you're inside.''

''What don't?'' Peter asked, desperate with anxiety.

"The engines. You can't 'ear them like you do when you're on the ground."

"Are you going to have a fit?" Peter asked.

Tommy looked down at his hands and finally answered. "I don't fink so."

Peter sighed with relief. "Are you scared?"

"Are you?"

"A bit. Bet you are too."

"A bit."

"What are we going to do?"

They looked down to the front of the plane and knew that unless the crew deliberately turned around or walked to the back they wouldn't know they were there. They could see the pilot at the controls and guessed the second pilot was sitting next to him and the navigator/wireless operator in his position behind the other two.

"See if there's anything written on the mail bags," Peter said and they dived down on to the bags searching for anything written on them.

"Look, Charleville!" Tommy cried.

"That's where we're going then."

"That's in England."

"Can't be." Peter grabbed the bag and pulled it flat. A large white "Q" stood out next to the name. "Queensland," he said, sighing with relief.

Tommy moved from the floor of the plane to the webbing seats along the side and Peter joined him. Tommy sat still, holding hard to the edge of the seat and Peter stood up and looked out of the window. Below he could see the patterns of fields, light green, dark green, bands of deep green trees, a dirt road cutting through the picture as though someone had drawn a line with a brown crayon.

Tommy gingerly stood up next to him, but drew back when he saw the earth so far below him. Then he came back and gazed at it all in wonder. Everything was so small. A tiny car on the road, a little doll's house on the side of the hill. A speck that must have been a boat on the tiny green river.

Looking straight in front of him, Peter spoke quietly. "It was my fault Charlie tipped over."

"I know that."

"Did you tell Grandad?"

"I don't blabber."

"Everything's changed since you came here."

"Would've changed anyway," Tommy told him.

They stood looking out through the windows, noticing that the sky had turned from blue to grey, that the sun had disappeared behind banks of greyness and they seemed to be flying right towards a high bank of grey and black clouds.

"We'd better tell them," Peter said and reluctantly Tommy nodded his head in agreement.

At the Air Force station at Tiboorie, a corporal walked down the path towards the hangars and saw two bikes. It seemed a strange place for anyone to have left them, but he didn't give much thought to it until he went back to the orderly room. He found Flight-Lieutenant Andrews gathering a group of men together to join in a search for his son and another boy who had been missing all the afternoon. "Went off somewhere on their bikes," he said.

The corporal took him out to the path near the trees and Flight-Lieutenant Andrews confirmed that one bike belonged to his son and the other must be Tommy Hooper's. He called for a staff car and drove to Charlie's house.

Flight-Lieutenant Andrews stood very tall in his Air

Force uniform, his cap under his arm, and talked to Charlie. As Charlie told Peter and Tommy afterwards, he had had no choice. Even he had begun to get worried. He told him that Peter had dared Tommy to get up close to an aeroplane because Peter thought he'd be too frightened to do it, but—he added quickly—it really was a good idea because it meant that Tommy would then be facing up to what scared him.

"I was the one who thought of that," Charlie added lamely.

Flight-Lieutenant Andrews got back into the car and drove to the airfield. He sat down at his desk for a few minutes, then lifted the receiver of his telephone.

It seemed hours to Tommy and Peter since the plane had left Tiboorie. Now they were cold and hungry and glad they'd made up their minds to tell the pilot. They slid off the seat, steadied themselves on the floor and were about to walk down the centre of the plane, as the pilot's voice boomed out through the doorway.

"Hey, are there two kids back there?"

The boys grabbed hold of the webbing seat.

The navigator took off his headphones, stood up and walked back to the body of the plane. He stopped when he saw them and ran his hand over his face and through his fair hair.

He turned back to the pilot. "Two boys. About twelve." And he led them back into the controls cabin. The pilot turned in his seat, took a quick look at them, grimaced, and looked away.

"How did you two get on board?" he asked, keeping his eyes on the wide clear window in front of him.

They stood together each wondering who was going to answer.

132

"It doesn't matter," the pilot said sharply, "don't answer that." He turned back to the navigator. "It's not getting any better down there, Ken," he said, ignoring Peter and Tommy. "That fog's just rolling in. Look at it."

The second pilot leaned to the side, looking down below him and the navigator walked back to his seat, put on the headphones and in a few moments said, "Archerfield closed. Fog in all areas."

"There goes our refuelling," the second pilot said half to himself.

"We'll make Charleville, just," the pilot breathed out. "That's if we get there before the fog."

Tommy and Peter looked out through the cockpit window. Everyone seemed to have forgotten about them. Below them billowing grey fog rolled over the land, blocking everything out as it went.

"Keep in touch with Charleville, Ken," the pilot ordered, "and, Ken, send out a message to Tiboorie. We've got those two kids they're looking for."

The two boys looked at each other wondering whether to go back to the body of the plane or stay where they were.

Then, "you boys, go back, sit down, and don't move," the pilot told them.

They sat on the webbing seat and listened to what was going on in the cabin. By leaning forward they could see the pilot and, as they knew where the second pilot sat and the navigator, they could tell which one was talking. The navigator kept listening to his wireless and relaying messages as he received them. It seemed that the fog was racing them towards Charleville. It was a battle to see which would get there first.

"Message from Charleville," the navigator reported. "Fog closing in. Divert to Longreach."

"Tell them we have to land at Charleville. We've only got fuel for ten minutes."

"Charleville's blotted out," the navigator reported, then added, "they're laying out a flare path."

"If we get down to 500 feet, should be able to see the airfield beacon and the flare-path," the second pilot said, searching down through the fog.

"Okay," the pilot's voice rang out, crisp and firm. "I'll take the controls, fly by instruments and keep at 500 feet until we find the flare-path. Don, you keep your eyes on the sky, on the ground and find a break in the fog or find the flare path. Ken, get behind me."

The navigator took off his headphones, replaced the fairly short cord with a longer one, and stood behind the pilot.

"Keep in touch with Charleville tower. Tell the operator to stand outside his radio room and listen for our engines. When he hears them tell him to radio to you a bearing and the approximate direction from the field."

A few moments of suspense and the pilot's steady voice rang out. "We're over Charleville. Can you see anything, Don?"

"Nothing."

The navigator's voice was less calm. He called. "He can hear us, we're north of the field."

The pilot pulled the plane around, banked and flew straight again. He turned around and barked, "you kids, come over here."

Peter and Tommy were beside him in a second.

"Look down there," he pointed, "straight ahead. Yell if you see any lights, if you see anything."

Everyone in the plane strained forward, gazing down at the spot where the airfield should be. The plane was flying at five hundred feet, the pilot preparing to land.

The navigator spoke slowly and clearly into his wireless

to the radio operator on the ground. "Can you hear our engines?"

"No."

"They must be able to hear us."

Tommy could feel the plane slowly descending. The engines throbbing steadily.

"Two hundred feet," the pilot snapped.

Tommy clutched the back of the pilot's seat and leaned forward, suddenly yelling. "Them's trees."

"Look out! Look out!" the second pilot shouted. "Pull up–up–up."

The boys hung on as the plane went up and levelled off.

"Full power." The pilot spoke softly now. "We'll go round again. Steady. Ask Charleville if they can hear our engines."

The navigator spoke into his microphone clamped on to his face. He moved it aside for a moment. "No, they can't," he said.

The pilot moved in his seat. "Keep looking for those lights, boys. Keep looking and yell when you see them."

The high pitched sound of the engine filled the aircraft while every eye stared out into the thick fog.

"There," Tommy yelled suddenly and pointed past the pilot's head to the east. "There!" Dim, hazy lights flickered through the dense fog. "Look, lights!"

"Right. Down on the floor. We're coming down. Two hundred feet, fifty feet."

Peter and Tommy flattened themselves on the hard floor. The wheels touched the ground. The plane bumped, lurched, rolled along and came to a screeching halt.

Tommy and Peter lay there, and when all the movement stopped they slowly rose to their feet.

The three men relaxed in their seats.

"I guess we're at Charleville," the pilot announced. Someone outside was banging on the door of the aircraft.

15   FACING THE MUSIC

The plane had overshot the runway. When they climbed down the steps they found they had landed in an open paddock, with trees down one side.

A car took them to the building behind the airstrip. An officer met them and they marched beside him to the office of the station's commanding officer.

The officer was angry, but to their surprise he didn't seem to be angry with them. His main concern seemed to be security and after he'd spoken on the telephone to the commanding officer at Tiboorie, he shouted at the sergeant sitting at a desk near the door.

"Letting two kids get on board an Air Force aircraft!" he fumed. "What were the guards doing? Sleeping?"

The sergeant took them to the dining mess to get something to eat then to the crew room where they sat down next to the three crew members.

"How about a lemonade?" the pilot asked.

For the first time Tommy and Peter relaxed.

They sat at a round table, sucking their lemonade through straws and watching the other men coming in and out. They were all officers. Some had pilot's wing insignia over the breast pockets of their jackets, others the one wing for navigator, or wireless air gunner.

"They're mostly visitors like us," the pilot told them. "Waiting to take off. We'll leave in the morning."

The navigator, Don leaned across the table and asked, "How did you come to get on the plane?"

Tommy waited for Peter to answer and Peter waited for Tommy.

"We didn't know it was going anywhere," Peter said at last.

"We just wanted to see it," Tommy explained.

"He wanted to." Peter pointed to Tommy. "He's scared of planes."

"Why are you scared of planes?" Don asked.

"Sounds as though he comes from England," the second pilot said, "that right?"

"Yes, he does." Peter took up the conversation. "He got bombed." He paused to sip some lemonade and as nobody said anything he went on. "His mum and sister got killed. The Germans did it." The men listened but made no comment. "So when he hears planes he thinks they're Germans and he has a fit."

Tommy squirmed in his seat. "I don't think they're Germans. I just hear the noise."

"And you think about what happened?" Don said gently.

"Yes."

Peter continued with his story seeing the airmen becoming more interested as he went on.

"Our schoolteacher wants to send him away to live somewhere else, but he wants to go to Africa."

Tommy kicked him fiercely under the table.

"Hold on now," the pilot said. "Why do you want to go to Africa, Tommy?"

Tommy lifted his head high when he answered. "Because my dad's there—fighting the Germans."

"Were you thinking of going there today?"

"No."

"He wants to go," Peter went on oblivious of Tommy's kicks, "but our mate Charlie wants him to stay and he said that if Tommy went up real close to an aeroplane and touched it even, he might get over his fits and things. I didn't think he'd be game."

Ken, the second pilot, joined in. "Well, he obviously was. I think he's a pretty game fellow."

The pilot looked at his watch. "We're almost out of time. What about another lemonade, then we'd better find beds for you."

Ken walked across to the counter and brought back two full glasses, and the pilot kept talking. "How do you feel about flying back to Tiboorie, Tommy?" he asked.

"It's all right." Tommy drank some lemonade and spoke half into his glass. "It's different when you're inside an aeroplane. The engines sound different."

"That's right. They do. How are you going to get to Africa?"

"Ship," Tommy replied.

"Ship?" The pilot repeated. "Stowaway?"

"Yes, I came out on a ship. I know 'ow to do it."

Peter rushed in. "We've got a friend called Alf— *ouch!*" He stopped in mid-sentence and rubbed his leg hard.

"Called what?" the pilot asked.

"Doesn't matter." Peter kept rubbing his leg and finished drinking his lemonade.

"Were you told about our passengers going back?"

The boys shook their heads.

"They've given us six stretcher cases from the hospital here. They need to go to Sydney for special treatment. We're taking them."

"What sort of stretcher cases?" Tommy asked.

"Blokes wounded up in New Guinea," the pilot

answered. "Come on, you'd better get some sleep. We leave at 0600 hours."

"What about if there's a fog?" Tommy asked.

"Getting up's not like getting down," he said. "Doubt if it'll be there but if it is we'll be out of it at a thousand feet."

They slept in a room by themselves on iron stretcher-beds, with grey heavy blankets. The window looked out over an asphalt parade ground.

"Looks like a prison," Tommy said, the legs of his borrowed pyjamas trailing down past his feet.

Peter rolled the sleeves of his up as high as he could, hobbled over to the bed and climbed in. Then he started to laugh.

"What's funny?" Tommy asked feeling too tired to worry.

"I was thinking about Charlie," he said. "He just wouldn't believe it if he could see us."

They both suddenly had a picture of the consternation they had caused at Tiboorie. Charlie waiting for them to come back, all the kids at school hearing about where they'd been.

"I 'ope Alfredo waits," Tommy said and in a few minutes they were asleep.

After a steaming hot breakfast they walked out with the three crew through the dim morning light to the plane. Inside they found two women in Air Force uniform standing between two tiers of stretchers strapped three on each side of the plane. Someone threw the steps on, closed the door and the crew sat in their seats ready for take-off. Tommy and Peter sat with the nursing sisters on the side seats, their seat-belts fastened.

The engines started, the plane taxied across the

tarmac, they waited and then the plane roared down the runway. They felt the lift as they took off into the air. In a short time the plane levelled and the nursing sisters undid their seat-belts and leaned across to undo the boys'.

Peter peered around the partition towards the crew and the navigator called out to him. "Okay, you can come in."

It took them only about three steps to get themselves once more standing behind the pilot's seat looking out at the wide open view in front of them.

"Do you think he was running away, Jack?" Mrs Walters asked for the third time as the taxi sped towards the airfield.

Charlie had told them about Peter daring Tommy to go and see the plane close up, but he hadn't said anything about Africa or Alfredo.

"No Marion," Mr Martin answered patiently. "He wouldn't have taken Peter with him if he'd been thinking of that. We won't know how it happened until we see them and ask."

At the station Flight-Lieutenant Andrews took them into his office and they sat down to wait, Mrs Walters with her handbag on her lap and her hands folded. Mr Martin crossed his legs and took out his pipe.

They listened while Peter's father explained what he knew had happened and sympathised with him when he told them that the whole station was in an uproar about the security and the cause of the whole trouble was his own son.

Jack Martin pressed the tobacco into his pipe. "I don't think you should be too hard on him, Ralph. He's probably learned his lesson."

"Well I hope he has," Flight-Lieutenant Andrews said

firmly. "And I certainly hope they're being properly punished out there in Charleville. They had no right, no right whatsoever to go into the hangar area. And Peter knew that. He's been given the privilege of coming and going here, seeing his friends in the married quarters, but not the hangars or the tarmac. He knows that."

Mrs Walters' voice wavered. "What kind of punishment? Proper punishment, you say."

"I know Doug Fisher, the pilot of that plane. He'll make sure they know what discipline means. He doesn't stand for nonsense."

He tidied his desk, moving papers from one side to the other, then picked up a pencil and began to write.

"They'll let us know when the plane lands."

Peter and Tommy looked out from behind the pilot's seat across a 180° expanse of wide open country. Tree covered mountains, patches of green fields in valleys, winding brown roads and the occasional car. Tommy could see the altimeter showing six thousand feet and looked at the other instruments to see whether he could work out what they were for.

The navigator was sitting back in his seat with his headphones on, an expression of calm and peace on his face—very different from the way he looked the night before. He took the headphones off and let them listen and to their surprise the only sound coming through was music.

"What are you listening to music for?" Peter asked. "We'll get lost."

"We're following the commercial radio stations," he explained. "That's the way we keep our bearings. We're heading straight for Sydney. Should be there in two hours."

The nursing sisters brought the crew some cocoa and Peter and Tommy went back with them into the plane for theirs.

The men lay on their stretchers quietly. Only one took a cup of cocoa, the others kept their eyes closed and didn't move.

Tommy asked the sister next to him about them, and she explained that they had all been wounded at Milne Bay.

"The first time we've been able to stop the Japs on the land," she told him.

"Were you in New Guinea?" Peter asked.

"We spend most of our time flying with the wounded back to Australia."

The man with the cocoa held out his empty cup and Tommy went over and took it. "What are you blokes doing here?" the soldier asked.

"It's a long story," Tommy began and he told him how it all happened.

"You've made my day," he said when Tommy finished. "Do you live in Tiboorie?"

They told him how Charlie would be waiting for them to get back, that his father had been reported missing in Singapore and that Tim had only been in the navy for a few months and now he'd probably be discharged.

"Doesn't know how lucky he is," the soldier told them.

"He doesn't think so," Peter assured him. "He'd rather be with my Uncle Bill. He came back from Africa and now he's gone to New Guinea. Do you know him? Bill Turner."

"What unit's he in?"

"Well, he's in the Sixth Division, I know that. I think he's in the 2/4th battalion."

"Well if he is he'll be up in the Owen Stanley Ranges. Poor cow."

The nurse came over to them. "That's enough talking," she said and tucked the blankets around her patient.

The pilot brought the cups back and stopped to look at each of the soldiers. When he went back to the controls he took the boys with them.

Instead of getting back into his seat he motioned to Tommy to sit down. Tommy's eyes widened, and gingerly he slid into the big padded seat beside the second pilot.

"How about doing a bit of flying?" the pilot said to him. "There you are. Take hold of the wheel. Hold it steady. That's right. Now turn it slightly left. Come back. Steady."

"Gee, you're flying the aeroplane," Peter shouted excitedly. "Can I have a go, Sir?"

Peter jumped from one foot to the other while he waited for Tommy to move and give him a turn. But Tommy stayed there, looking out in front of him, watching the instruments and listening to the pilot explain the way it all worked. At last Tommy stood up and Peter sighed a deep sigh of contentment as he settled behind the controls himself. He too was flying a plane.

In Sydney orderlies came on board and carried the wounded off. The nursing sisters put on their coats, collected their bags and followed them, giving both boys a kiss on the cheek as they stepped out on to the steps.

Men on the tarmac refuelled the plane and in a short time they were airborne again.

The water of Sydney Harbour shone below them and Tommy gasped in amazement. "It didn't look like that when we came in in the ship," he said. "Where's Garden Island?"

The navigator pointed it out to them and they told him about Tim.

Then they circled and flew off west towards Tiboorie. As they got closer they began to recognise landmarks and they came in over the top of the post office, landed at the airfield and taxied across the tarmac towards the hangars.

They climbed down the steps with the crew and for a moment forgot about the reception that must be waiting for them at the station.

Peter walked close to the pilot as they entered the administrative building and held on to the sleeve of his coat.

"Do you think we'll be skinned alive?" he asked.

"Could be," the pilot replied. "Commanding officers don't take too kindly to stowaways on planes."

"But what about fathers?" Peter asked. "That's what I'm worrying about."

Mrs Walters smothered Tommy with kisses when he finally came into the room where she waited. Jack Martin put his arm around Peter and looked him over carefully.

"You all right, son?" he asked, his voice husky.

Flight-Lieutenant Andrews stood at his desk, glaring.

"Hello, Dad," Peter said.

Mrs Walters and Mr Martin sat down and the two boys stood in front of the desk. He waited for a few moments and then he began to talk.

"I'm not going to wait to talk to you," he said. "I'm going to talk now and you listen. Listen to every word I have to say."

They listened to him and after a few minutes they began to wish they had never thought of the idea of going into the hangar. But as the voice from behind the desk continued, their minds went back to the way the door had slammed when they were hiding in the mail bags; how the engines started up; coming down in the fog; finding the flare strip; the wounded soldier they talked to on the way back; the nursing sisters; the pilot and Don and Ken. And they had flown the plane. Flight-Lieutenant Andrews stopped talking and they blinked their eyes back into the present.

"So what I am asking you to do, is think," they heard him say. "Think before you act. Think it through. Then you won't get yourselves involved in any more dangerous escapades like this one. We try to protect you, but you've got to go half way."

It was over. They all piled into the taxi and drove home. Peter and Tommy sat in the back and, when Mr Martin stopped and opened the car door for Mrs Walters, Peter moved into the front and wound down the window.

"When are you going to see Alfredo?" he asked, as quietly as he could.

"Soon as I can," Tommy answered.

"Don't go anywhere without telling us," he said, "Charlie and me."

He waved as Tommy went inside with his aunt and the car drove off.

Mrs Walters put on the kettle and reached for the biscuit tin.

"I'm not going to talk much," she told him, "Mr Andrews did enough of that. There's just one thing I want to know, Tommy. One thing to put my mind at rest."

Tommy took a biscuit and waited for her to go on. She seemed sad and lonely. Different from the way he had expected.

"Were you really running away, Tommy?"

He knew he could answer her question truthfully. No he wasn't. But he also knew it was only half the truth. "Miss Leslie wants me to go away," he told her.

"I know. But that's not an answer. Were you running away?"

"No."

She closed her eyes and breathed in deeply. "I've thought about it all, Tommy. Miss Leslie thinks a psych—psychiatrist would help you and they're only in big cities. Like Sydney. I should go with you, Tommy. Take you there if it'll help. But I can't do that. I have to keep the garage going and the shop—for Bert. I promised him when he went away. I can't leave here, Tommy."

He picked up his biscuit but found he couldn't eat, so put it back on the table. "When's Miss Hume comin'?"

"Monday."

She poured the boiling water from the kettle into the teapot and put it on the table. As she passed him she bent down and kissed him and he knew the wetness he felt on his cheek were her tears.

"I won't let them send you anywhere, Tommy. Not if you want to stay. You and I will fight it out together. We can manage. You're here with me and that's where you're going to stay. We don't need a psych—oh, drat that word!"

In the afternoon Tommy rode up to the farm half expecting that Alfredo would not be there. But he found Mr Turner, Alfredo and Jo in the dairy and they welcomed him as though they hadn't seem him for weeks.

"Stirred the whole town up like a stick in a beehive," Mr Turner joked. "What got into the two of you?"

Tommy wanted to get away and talk to Alfredo, but he answered Mr Turner as best he could and waited till Alfredo and Jo finished the milking.

They walked down to the barn and sat on the boxes outside the door.

"Alfredo?" Tommy asked without wasting any time, "what about your plan? When are you going?"

"All has changed." Alfredo moved his foot on the dry

dirt in front of him. "I no go to Italy." He put his hand on his chest. "My heart is broke."

"You're not going at all?" Tommy wanted to make quite sure.

"I stay here."

"I'm not going to Africa either. I was going, but I couldn't find you to tell you. I wanted to go with you."

They both sat silently and Jo looked across from one to the other wondering what they had said to make them both look so sad.

"Giovanni stay. When the war is ended we work here on the farm. No more Italy."

Giovanni heard his name mentioned and nodded in agreement.

"You?" Alfredo asked. "When the war is ended you go to England?"

Tommy hadn't thought that far ahead. The war had been going on since he was nine. It didn't seem to him that it would ever finish and he hadn't thought of what he would do when it did. It would depend who won—the Germans and the Japanese or the British and the Americans. There might not be any England left to go to. Now that he wasn't going to Africa he would write to his father and tell him to come to Australia. Then there would be no need to go back to England. But it was all too far ahead to think about. His worry was what was happening now.

After a while he said goodbye and went back to his bike. Mrs Turner called out to him from the separating room and he went in and watched her turning the handle.

"I'll get you a jar of cream to take back to your auntie," she said. "A meal's not the same without a bit of cream. Heard you'd been on a bit of an adventure, Tommy. Doesn't sound to me that you'll be too worried about planes now. Not after that."

He carried the cream in its jar tucked down inside his

shirt and pedalled back, thinking over what Mrs Turner had said. He didn't feel scared. It was great thinking about the things he had done with Peter. But the most important thing was whether Peter still thought he was a coward. He didn't think he would, but he hadn't said.

He stopped outside Charlie's house and went inside and when he'd finished telling his story Charlie looked at him, his eyes wide with admiration. "Gee, it's true then—what you and Peter did?"

"Of course it is."

"My idea worked then. Gosh, I reckon I'm pretty clever."

At home Tommy noticed the two empty tea cups as soon as he walked into the kitchen and knew his aunt had had a visitor.

As soon as she'd put the cream away she turned to him and beamed. "I've had a visitor." She glowed with pleasure, but he had no idea who she meant. "A friend of yours."

"Mine. Who's that then?"

"Flying Officer Fisher."

He was more surprised than he could imagine. The pilot. Why had he come? And he'd missed seeing him.

"He wanted to know more about you. And I told him. Told him all about that Miss Leslie and we know exactly what we're going to do. We've got a very busy time ahead of us, Tommy Hooper, but we've got the guns out now, and we're going to start firing."

16   TIBOORIE DECIDES

On Monday morning at eleven o'clock Jack Martin picked up Miss Hume from the Sydney train. When Mrs Walters opened her front door he came inside with them and they all walked into the lounge together.

Flying Officer Fisher stood up as they came and Miss Hume shook hands with him, her astonishment showing clearly as she murmured, "How do you do."

She turned to Mrs Walters apologetically. "I did think, Mrs Walters, that our appointment meant we'd talk together alone. Perhaps we could go into the—"

Flying Officer Fisher interrupted. "Tommy's problem is a shared one, Miss Hume. Mr Martin here and I both feel there's a lot that should be said. There are a great many people in Tiboorie who feel that Tommy would be much better off if he stayed here. Planes or no planes."

"That's hardly a matter for the people of Tiboorie to decide," she told him icily. "One must have a clear analytical view of these problems, not emotional."

The doorbell rang and Mrs Walters excused herself and went down the hall to answer it. Flight-Lieutenant Andrews came in with Mrs Andrews, Pam and Mrs Calder. She introduced them to Miss Hume.

148

They crowded into the room and the doorbell rang again.

"Really," Miss Hume fumed, "this is entirely unnecessary, Mrs Walters. All we needed was a quiet—"

"I'll answer it," Jack Martin called, dashing off down the hallway. "Then I'll be off to the school to pick up Miss Leslie and Tommy. You wanted to see them, didn't you, Miss Hume?" he asked innocently.

She stammered a reply as he opened the door for Mr and Mrs Turner, Alfredo and Jo.

Peter and Charlie arrived on their bikes as Jack left and along the road he passed Tim walking towards the shop. He felt a sudden pang of sadness for Tim as he remembered that his discharge from the Navy had been confirmed. That elbow was never going to be quite right again.

Peter and Charlie were parking their bikes just as an Air Force car pulled up. The second pilot, Ken, and the navigator, Don, jumped out and Peter introduced Charlie.

"Got a bit of a conference going," Don said smiling. "Two votes coming in."

By now people were packed into the house like sardines.

Miss Hume sat in her chair tapping her fingers on the arm rest. "We'll wait until Miss Leslie arrives," she told Mrs Walters, "then whoever wants to speak can do so."

Flying Officer Fisher replied. "Mightn't be a bad idea to let Tommy say a few words. He seems to know what he wants."

"What he wants, Flying Officer Fisher, and what is best for him, are, I believe, two different things. A little boy, psychologically distressed by the events that have happend to him, is living in a town within two miles of an Air Force station. It seems to me that Miss Leslie is quite right to be concerned. It is completely unfair to the boy."

They heard the taxi pull up outside and the doors slam.

Miss Leslie, Jack Martin and Tommy squeezed their way into the room.

Miss Leslie looked at the crowded lounge in amazement, then down the hall to the kitchen, and out the window. Another group of people stood bunched together outside.

"I suppose you all think that Tommy should stay in Tiboorie," she said.

Don the navigator put his head around the doorway. "We could take a vote on it."

Miss Hume had been sitting at a table in the middle of the room. Now she picked up her briefcase, opened it and took out a sheaf of papers and a pen. "This is most unusual," she told them, and putting on her glasses began to read the top paper.

"Tommy's not on trial," she said at last. "This isn't a court room. I merely have to satisfy myself that Tommy will be all right if he stays here, and put in a report."

Jack Martin stepped forward a pace. "And we're here to convince you he *is* all right and should stay."

She took off her glasses and put down her pen. "It would take all day to listen to what each of you has to say," she said to them, "so there's really only one person I would like to hear from."

Tommy felt his knees shake. She was going to ask him and somehow he had to tell her that he wasn't scared any more, that as many aeroplanes as they liked could fly over the town and he wouldn't shake. He just knew it. Everyone had come because they wanted him to stay. He would never be scared again, knowing that.

But Miss Hume looked down at her notes, then looked right over Tommy's head to Peter. "The boy who went with Tommy in the plane,'' she said, ''Peter, Peter Andrews. What do you think, Peter?''

''Me?''

His grandfather moved him forward until Peter stood in front of them all—his schoolteacher Miss Leslie and the person he'd never seen before, Miss Hume, the pilot, the second pilot, the navigator and all the Tiboorie people. And Alfredo and Jo.

''Well. . .'' He shuffled his feet. ''Well. . .'' He ran his tongue around his dry lips. ''He's scared of cows and he can't swim and he's not much good at football. . .'' He stopped and looked at the faces waiting for him to go on. ''But he can fly an aeroplane and he's *not* scared of them—not any more, he isn't.''

''Do you think Tommy would be able to manage if he stayed in Tiboorie?''

Peter looked at Tommy standing squashed between the pilot and Miss Hume. He's a funny looking kid, he thought. It seemed years since they'd first seen him on the train at the crossing. He knew they could never go back to the time before Tommy came. Everything had changed, but it wasn't Tommy's fault. He felt differently about a lot of things now.

''What do you think, Peter?'' Miss Hume asked again.

''He'll be all right,'' he said and felt the crowd around him relax. A few clapped and then someone cheered and gradually the cheers and the clapping filled all the rooms of the house and almost lifted the corrugated iron roof off the building.

''Well. . . if everyone will give me some room,'' Miss Hume called loudly, ''I'll write out my report and get back to Sydney.''

Peter's birthday fell on a Sunday and he and his grand-father went down to the park with Charlie and Tommy to fly the model aeroplane Charlie had given him.

Tim came too, in ''civvies'', and Pam came, and they all raced back and forth across the grass chasing the plane.

When it landed near Tommy, Peter watched him pick it up, retwist the rubber band around its propellor and throw it high into the air. He didn't seem to notice the DC3 flying over his head—just raced after the model plane, picked it up when it landed and handed it to Peter. It was his turn. Peter threw it back into the air as the DC3 disappeared from sight on its way south.